FREE TO ACT:

HOW TO STAR IN YOUR OWN LIFE

FREE TO ACT:

HOW TO STAR IN YOUR OWN LIFE

by Warren Robertson

G. P. Putnam's Sons
New York

The author and publishers gratefully acknowledge permission to quote passages from:

A Doll's House by Henrik Ibsen, translated by R. Farquharson Sharp. An Everyman's Library edition. Published in the United States by E. P. Dutton & Co., Inc. and reprinted with their permission.

Desire Under the Elms, from SELECTED PLAYS BY EUGENE O'NEILL, copyright 1969 by Random House, Inc.

Mademoiselle Colombe by Jean Anouilh, adapted by Louis Kronenberger. Copyright 1954 by Jean Anouilh and Louis Kronenberger and reprinted by permission of Coward, McCann & Geoghegan, Inc.

Miss Julie, from SIX PLAYS BY STRINDBERG by August Strindberg, translated by Elizabeth Sprigge. Copyright 1955 by Elizabeth Sprigge and reprinted by permission of Curtis Brown, Ltd.

Scenes From American Life by A. R. Gurney, Jr. Copyright 1970 by A. R. Gurney, Jr. Used by permission of The Sterling Lord Agency, Inc.

Saint Joan by George Bernard Shaw. Reprinted by permission of The Society Of Authors on behalf of the Bernard Shaw Estate.

Enemies by Maxim Gorky. Translation copyright 1972 by Kitty Hunter-Blair and Jeremy Brooks. Reprinted by permission of The Viking Press.

Who's Afraid of Virginia Woolf by Edward Albee. Copyright 1962. Reprinted by permission of Atheneum, Publishers.

Cyrano de Bergerac by Edmond Rostand, translated by Brian Hooker. Copyright 1923 by Holt, Rinehart, & Winston. Copyright 1951 by Doris C. Hooker. Reprinted by permission of Holt, Rinehart & Winston.

SBN: 0-399-11961-2

Library of Congress Cataloging in Publication Data

Robertson, Warren.
    Free to act: how to star in your own life.

    1. Success. 2. Role playing. 3. Personality change. I. Title.
BF637.S8R58   1977   158'.1   77-3616

PRINTED IN THE UNITED STATES OF AMERICA

I want to express my appreciation to David Fisher, without whose efforts this book would not have been possible.

I would also like to acknowledge the valuable contributions and support of John Milton Williams, Victoria Tarlow, Anita Elliot, Tom Epstein, Bernie Sohn, Maureen McCluskey, Lane Yorke, Hank Berrings, Dr. Lester Coleman, Sally Andrews, Diane Matthews, David Smith, Frank Bowers, Dell Martin, Rita Elgar, William Horne, Joe Daly, John Boswell, Jim Moran, Pat Terry, and Gene Barracat.

To my daughters, Cara and Gina, and all my family

CONTENTS

CHAPTER ONE:
The Longest Running Play in Town—Your Life

Men are free to act, but must act to be free.

—JEAN-PAUL SARTRE

Once upon a time in your life anything was possible. You were free to take almost any actions you desired. You were free to imagine the most wonderful possibilities. But as you grew older and acquired responsibilities, much of this freedom was lost. Your childhood dreams were shattered by the hammers of reality. So many obstacles came between your desires and your ability to fulfill them that you began to settle. And settle. And you learned how to settle. Those countless options you once had no longer existed. Your life was out of your own control. And now you feel trapped, inadequate, defeated. Meaningful change no longer seems possible. You no longer imagine wild possibilities. You feel you are a failure at life.

Or worse, you feel nothing at all.

9

Your life doesn't have to be this way. There need be no more one single confining role in your life than there is a single role for an actor. Just as Marlon Brando can become a punch-drunk dockworker in one film, a Mexican bandit in a second, and an aged Mafia godfather in a third, change is always possible.

I know this for certain because I have been teaching acting—the fine art of taking actions—for more than fifteen years. In that time I have taught over 10,000 men and women. Many of my present and former students are working actors and actresses who are currently in starring or supporting roles in major motion pictures or legitimate theatre. Several have been awarded or been nominated for the top awards that Hollywood and Broadway have to offer. I have taught acting to people from virtually every profession and walk of life. Among my "alumni" are some of the most beautiful models in the world, many professional athletes, including a contender for the heavyweight boxing title, secretaries, policemen, waitresses, construction workers, taxi drivers, housewives—young or old, rich or poor, of every race and creed.

I've discovered that all of my students have one thing in common: the ability to change. Change is always possible. It is an ability never lost. No matter how trapped you may feel right now, no matter how burdened with responsibilities, no matter how resigned to your life you've become, change is absolutely possible.

The method that I've developed to teach actors will work for you. Performers are simply human beings who happen to work in a glamorous field. The material I work with and try to shape in each one of them is the same basic material you bring to every moment in your life: your body, mind, and emotions.

The principal difference between you and these performers is that their profession allows them to concentrate on developing this basic material. Acting demands that they bring total attention and awareness to every part of themselves. And, unlike any other profession, acting gives human beings an opportunity to rehearse for life.

In learning his craft, the actor must deal with every aspect of the composition of life. He must become aware of every part of himself, his dress, manner of speaking, the way he relates to other people, his posture, attitudes, disposition, even the many different ways he might comb his hair. He must permit himself to experience the entire range of human emotions he might someday have to duplicate: joy, fear, sorrow, love, pain, anguish, anxiety, depression, and the multitude of others. And he must learn to consider all the options available to him at any moment and how to make the best possible decision based on his knowledge of his own capabilities.

In a sense, you are an actor. You have been cast in a role in the longest running play in town, your life. It may not be the role you once dreamed of playing, and you may have never auditioned for it, but somehow you wake up each morning to find yourself preparing to play your character. An agent at one of the major talent agencies, and later a student in my workshop, once confided that he spent 90 percent of his time putting together a character for the rest of the world, and the other 10 percent of his time despising that character.

How did you end up cast in your particular role? It would be impossible to enumerate all the things that have influenced you.

An enormously talented actress stood on the stage at my acting studio, looked down upon twenty-five other students and she announced somberly, "I'm not here."

The class laughed, but I realized she was absolutely serious. Knowing that events from the past often project themselves into the present, I asked, "Then where are you?"

The class became totally silent. She stood frozen on the stage, her legs just slightly starting to shiver.

I suggested, "Why don't you make a long-distance call inside yourself and find out where you are?"

She paused. Her face began to tremble. "I'm in the second grade at school. And I'm reading my poetry."

"Please look directly at the class when you are talking," I said. I waited as she lowered her eyes and made eye contact. "How do you feel?"

Her chin started to droop. She looked ashamed, like a sorrowful little girl. "Everyone's laughing at me and I'm reading my beautiful poetry." Suddenly she burst into tears. "They're laughing at me. I don't want them to laugh. I want to make them cry with my beautiful words."

As a second grader, the pain and humiliation she experienced forced her to make a choice, either retreat inside herself and become completely shut off, or take the laughter as acceptance. At least they laughed. She started trying to be a funny person, but a funny person with a sad face. She was a pouting little girl. At that moment, as a child, she was cast into the role of the clown, the comic.

But once she began to understand that she had grown up playing the role developed by a frightened child, she began to change. Her capacity for serious work expanded. Her few extra pounds, part of her funny-little-girl disguise, quickly disappeared. Soon after, she was cast into a major motion picture and won the first of two Academy Award nominations.

This book is based on the technique I've developed and shaped during my career as both a performer and actor, the same technique I used when working with this actress. It is about acting, the fine art of taking actions in the world. It is a method which requires the actor to grow as a person and to explore his complete potential, and it is as applicable to your world as it is to that of the performer. This method is based on a series of exercises that, carefully followed, will reintroduce you to the different parts of your body and the

FREE TO ACT   13

world around you and enable you to initiate actions and thus regain the freedom to make choices and important changes in your life.

The exercises in this book are part of an entire program. They are rehearsals for life. They will introduce you to new forms of behavior that, with enough practice, will become ingrained in your everyday life.The program consists of simple tasks that require you to bring your full awareness to different parts of your body, mind, and emotions. Much of your behavior has become habitual; you do things simply because you're used to doing them. Often, in fact, you're not even consciously aware that you're doing these things. The exercises will show you how much of your life is habitual. They will help open your life to new possibilities, and allow you to become free enough to make real choices. They will help you take control of your own life.

I am an acting teacher. The purpose of my work is to prepare people to utilize their abilities to become successful performers. I don't accept students into my workshop unless they are serious about working in acting. But I discovered long ago that training an actor involves far more than teaching basic theatre techniques. Complete training includes giving a person back the capacity to feel and the capacity to express those feelings to the world.

Acting without feeling is like singing without music. It lacks support. It lacks resonance. It lacks richness. Usually critics describe it as "flat"; the audiences are usually bored. But on those occasions when an actor communicates intense feeling, the theatre seems to crackle with electricity. It is that way in life, too. Many people are pleasant enough, but go through life making no impact on their surroundings. Others simply step into a room and they dominate the scene. They are described as "dynamic," or said to have "charisma." What is it that makes the difference? At least part of it is the ability to communicate honest emotions to other people, through the body, voice, and the spoken word.

Everybody has feelings. At some point in your life you have experienced the incredible range of emotions from euphoria to depression. But many people, and you may be among them, have learned to hide, or disguise, these real feelings. They have replaced them with socially acceptable emotions. In the never-ending quest to be liked, and loved, they have limited their feelings to those that make other people comfortable. The supporting cast is writing the script of life.

There is a popular notion today that if an individual can be free to laugh and cry, feel anger, rage, joy, pain, and pleasure, somehow she or he will have a totally fulfilling life. Unfortunately this is not completely true. Experiencing your deep feelings is no more the total solution to life than it is to acting. Feeling does not make a complete person— the feelings have to be translated into actions. The feelings are only the material for life, they are the support, the fuel, the motivation for effective actions.

A great deal of my preliminary class work, and much of the exercise work in this book, involves getting "in touch" with your feelings, but that is only the preliminary work. That feeling must be communicated to the world. You must use it. And that is done by choosing, and taking, actions.

For the actor, choosing actions based on real feelings translates into an exciting, believable characterization. For you, being able to experience real feelings and express them to the rest of the world through actions will lead to a much more satisfying life. You will be able to choose actions that fulfill your needs and desires. You will be free to act.

I first began to realize that the same techniques used to train an actor might be applied to creating a more healthy, satisfying, and effective way of life. While studying at a famed actor's studio in New York, among the people in my class were such celebrated performers as Marilyn Monroe, James Dean, Inger Stevens, Peter Falk, Tony Franciosa, and Rip Torn. These were all people at the height of their success, the best actors in the business.

One afternoon Inger Stevens was doing a stretching exercise. As she lifted her hands high above her head, the sleeves of her sweater slid down her forearms, revealing thick bandages taped around both wrists. The day before she had attempted to kill herself. But no one in class said a word to her about it. No one knew how to deal with this incredible fact. The stretching exercises continued. Two months later Inger Stevens committed suicide.

It was evident to me that an intelligent woman like Inger Stevens had intense feelings flowing inside her. But what I later understood was that she had no means of communicating them to the world. Her body had lost contact with her feelings and she could not express them. Her emotions went as far as her wrists and throat, then stopped. They were locked in. She didn't know how to express them either verbally or through her body. It occurred to me that this is precisely the reason people commit suicide by cutting their wrists, as Inger Stevens finally did, or by hanging themselves.

Actors are able to create real characters, characters who came alive on stage or in films. They learn to bring real emotion to their roles, and express it to the audience. Yet some of them simply cannot apply that same insight to their own lives. In real life, Inger Stevens could not communicate the pain she was feeling, the hurt that led to her taking her life. The same was true of James Dean and, later, Marilyn Monroe.

At the studio we were spending a great amount of time learning how to examine a character. We were learning how to take a character apart piece by piece, examine each part, work specifically to develop and improve each part, and finally bring them all together to create a complete, believable character. We could create happy characters, sad characters, intense, crazy or violent characters, but we were ignoring our real selves and the problems we had as human beings. It occurred to me that we were not sufficiently bringing our awareness to the original material we brought to this creation. After watching Inger Stevens destroy herself, I could see no reason why the same exercises we used to understand a character couldn't be applied to examining and improving ourselves.

At that time, my deep conviction of the intimate relationship between theatre and life began. Theatre is about life. It is about people in conflict. It is a composition of situations, condensed and organized, and the struggle of characters to resolve conflict. The audience goes to the theatre to see if there is perhaps a better way to understand and solve life's problems—to see how Hamlet or Willy Loman or Hedda Gabler deal with universal themes. The characters take actions against opposition, whether it is another human being, the terrain, or the elements, and attempt to turn adversity to their advantage.

Actors thus have the opportunity to explore almost limitless possibilities and situations, behave in various ways, confront numerous obstacles, and take steps to resolve dramatic conflicts. They are allowed to prepare for these characterizations in many ways. They can rehearse by stepping in and out of the role; they can take a break from the intensity of conflict, exercise the various parts, attempt different actions until they find the proper one, or experiment with different props. They can bring the entire range of their imagination to each moment, and do all this with impunity, because they do not permanently become their character.

Many people become actors because of this freedom of expression. While real life confines them to a limited number of exploits, dimensions, and feelings, the stage allows them to explore endless possibilities. Often the things an actor wins acclaim for are the very things that would be condemned in real life. Thus Shirley Jones can win an Academy Award for her portrayal of a prostitute in *Elmer Gantry*. And the late Peter Finch can also receive the Academy Award for his creation of a newsman going berserk on national television in *Network*. Al Pacino worked his way up from a gay bank robber in *Dog Day Afternoon* to the top of organized crime in *The Godfather*, then turned completely around to become the honest cop, *Serpico*. Sylvester Stallone's rags-to-riches *Rocky* allowed him to utilize his boxing expertise, as well as his firsthand knowledge of what life is like when you're on the bottom struggling for a break. Acting permits the performer to play.

Unfortunately, you may believe that this freedom to play, to change roles and become different characters, is limited to trained actors. Instead of an endless series of meaty roles, you see yourself cast as one character for the entire run of your life-play, with no hope of changing the script, the setting, or the cast of supporting characters. You may have accepted the fact that you will spend your life in a very local production of *Our Town*.

It doesn't have to be that way. An actor can change roles and plays, and so can you. Just as the actor has the ability to try different approaches, to experiment, to change his stage life by changing roles, you have the freedom to write yourself a new role, with new actions, intentions, and a brand-new plot line. Few actors are willing to sign long-term contracts committing them to one role because they've learned that any part can eventually become confining and boring, yet many people willingly spend their lives in a role they find unfulfilling because they have either never learned, or else they have forgotten, that they are free to act.

We are all actors, born into long-running plays. Often we never even audition for another role, simply because we come to believe we are in the only show in town. The play I was born into was set in a small southwest Texas town named Archer City. All the roles in this play were firmly established. The leading players were the ranchers and oil men, and they had total control over the script. They determined the social structure, ran the school system, controlled the merchant businesses. The roles never changed. If a member of the cast had to be replaced, usually because of death or retirement, his stand-in, his son or chosen successor, would step into his costume without missing a line. The rest of the cast of the "Archer City Story," about nine hundred people, played all the supporting and bit roles. Although I didn't realize it at the time, various adaptations of this play were running all over the country.

My father was a feature player. He filled whatever role was available, the friendly bartender, the hardworking auto mechanic, the loyal oil field hand. Growing up in Archer City, I never realized I had any options. The role I coveted was the star of the high school football team. After that I would take my place in the cast among the supporting players. This play had been written long before I was born, and there seemed to be no escape from the sociological central casting.

The most important building in that old town was the tiny movie house, the Royal Theatre. It seated only about fifty people and had a small screen, but it was our lifeline to the rest of the world. Eventually my schoolmate, Larry McMurty, would immortalize the Royal, Archer City, and our seventeen-member high school graduating class in his remembrance, *The Last Picture Show*. In the darkness of that theatre, the audience would allow themselves to release all the pent-up emotions their roles as respectable citizens prohibited them from expressing. They would scream at the actors, shout warnings, sympathize loudly, hoot during love scenes, argue, and cheer. The dark of the Royal set them free to play, to live vicariously through the movies, to finally let their real feelings loose. Often people would get so involved in the action of the movie they would throw something, an apple or a shoe, through the screen. By the end of the picture the leading man was nothing but a shoulder, his head disappearing into a dark hole.

One of the great awakenings of my life took place in the Royal. I had been brought up to believe that people were unable to change their characters. Life roles were carefully etched; there were good people and bad people, rich people and poor people, happy people and sad people, just like in the movies. The men I saw in Archer City were certainly all one way, they were fixed into types, hardened into a single part. I assumed everyone in the world could only be one way. Pug-faced Edward G. Robinson helped teach me differently.

I remember fearing him as Rico, the essential tough guy, in *Little Caesar,* and hating him as a venal character in *Key Largo.* Then, unexpectedly, in *Our Vines Have Tender Grapes*, he was warm, gentle, and paternal with the little girl, Margaret O'Brien. I was overwhelmed when I realized Edward G. Robinson could be tough or warm, and still be accepted by the audience. People could change characters and still be accepted; human beings did have the ability to be flexible. For the first time I was aware that I didn't have to play one role for the rest of my life. Change was possible. This was quite a great discovery for a child to make. All I knew was that, somehow, change was possible. I had no idea how to begin that change.

Somehow Larry McMurty also made this discovery, and while we wanted to change our roles, other members of the Archer City cast had their parts changed by the course of events. When World War II began, men who would have otherwise never traveled beyond the big cities like Austin and Amarillo were suddenly being sent all over the world.

They returned to Texas bursting with fantastic stories about exotic places like California, Waynesville, Missouri, and Fort Dix, New Jersey, as well as absolutely unbelievable places like France, Italy, and the Far East. Through their stories, hundreds of different plays and countless roles were revealed to me. I wouldn't have to play my part as a pickup truck driver on a ranch in west Texas. As Blanche DuBois understood in Tennessee Williams's *A Streetcar Named Desire*, that knowledge was "like a blinding light shining on something that had always been half in shadow for me."

Without even realizing it, many people live out their lives playing character parts in their local version of my home-town play. They are not even aware that change is possible, so they will never attempt it.

I repeat: change is always possible.

You begin with the knowledge that it is possible. Often, that awareness is all that is needed to cause change. Once you understand that you behave in a certain way, it becomes possible to change the way you behave.

Certain behavior patterns might not need changing at all. Instead you might simply need to bring your self-awareness up to date. One of my students was chosen to test for the lead role of "Prewitt" in a proposed television series based on James Jones's *From Here to Eternity.* He is a strikingly handsome, muscular actor who was physically perfect for the part of the sensitive boxer. However, throughout his audition, he had trouble playing scenes which required him to be forceful or commanding. There was no real reason for this: he looked forceful and commanding, and he is a quite capable actor.

The problem, as we discovered through the exercise work, was caused by the fact that he was not really aware of himself. As a child he had been so slender friends had nicknamed him "Spider," and warned him never to take a shower without putting the stopper in or he'd slip down the drain. Although he filled out as he grew, he was never really aware that he had changed physically. In his mind he was still skinny "Spider," still taking actions that would be correct for a tall, thin, somewhat shy person. His reticent behavior was totally incongruous with his strong appearance.

By utilizing simple exercises to focus his attention on the man he had become, practicing different actions, he was able to overcome that childhood casting and win the part. Although that show never made it on the air, he later starred in the successful western series, "Alias Smith and Jones."

Like this actor, many people are unaware of the appearance they present to the rest of the world. Some even continue to take the same actions that were successful for them as early as high school for the remainder of their lives, and never understand why they no longer achieve the same success they did as a teenager.

The answer, of course, is that they have become a different person. The actions that are successful for a pubescent cheerleader are embarrassing when taken by an overwieght middle-aged woman. As we grow, we all change physically and emotionally. Unfortunately, many people become psychologically fixed at a point in their lives and stop growing. They are not even aware of who they really are.

The first exercise allows you to focus complete attention on your most basic behavior. It is simple and involves no preparation. It is designed to make you more aware of yourself. Relax, keep your eyes open, and begin.

BREATH: AWARENESS

The first exercise is the focusing of all your attention on your breathing. Breathing is the basis of life. You can survive days or weeks without food or water, but only about three minutes without breathing. Yet how long has it been since you were aware of your breathing process. Feel your breath go in. Is it cold? Warm? Feel your chest expand, then depress. Listen to the sound your body makes. When your complete attention is focused on your breathing, you are "with" your breath. Notice the attention you are directing to this part of yourself is slightly different than usual. You should "let go" of awareness of everything else around you and concentrate on your breathing. It should be very relaxing, calming.

You may have never willfully concentrated your complete attention on a part of yourself in this way before. If so, this is a new awareness. You have experienced your body and your world in a totally new way. Later in this book you will be asked to bring this complete attention to other parts of your body and environment. You will be shown how to make yourself more aware of who you really are and the world that surrounds you.

Take a deep breath. Release it.

I begin with your breath because it is the starting point of life. Everything else about you may change, but your breathing will always remain a fixed point to return to at any time. In the midst of the most outrageously frightening experience or a time of great depression or joy, you can always bring your attention to your breathing and find this starting place. It is permanent, reliable, constant.

Normally you are not "with" you breath or any part of your body or environment. In fact, unless you have studied some form of meditation or have a respiratory problem, you are very rarely aware of your breathing. This is also true for your other parts and your environment. Unless there is some compelling reason to bring your attention to a place or moment, you are probably being carried along automatically on the wave of day-to-day events and problems of life.

Again: breathe in, easily, and out.

Please stop the first exercise now.

Notice, you are still breathing. The breathing exercise is important for two reasons. It is a simple way of introducing the method of concentrating your awareness, which will be important in later exercises, and it allows you to bring all your attention to the single fixed point that will always be available to you. At any time, no matter how much everything about you changes, you can return to the starting point.

Once more, bring all your attention to this exercise. Take a deep breath. Hold it. Feel your abdomen fill. And release the breath.

Awareness exercises, the focusing of concentrated attention, are the beginning of change. But awareness is not change. It is, instead, preparation for taking actions to make changes. Building a tunnel is not an escape; it is a means to escape. In the same way, awareness exercises are a means to begin effecting change.

Awareness alone is not enough. You may be aware that change is desirable, but simply not know how to do anything about it. That feeling of being trapped leads to enormous frustration, very often manifested by bitterness. At the end of World War II, for example, most Archer City natives who marched off to war returned home. The town was much the same as they had left it. The play was still running strong and their parts had been held open for them. And although almost everyone slipped back into the cast, many of the men were never again satisfied with that small town.

Awareness that other roles existed wasn't enough for the soldiers. They did not have the ability to act on that knowledge. They remained in the same old play, but they were no longer comfortable. Knowing that other opportunities existed but not knowing how to take advantage of them caused great discontent. They felt trapped.

Awareness pinpoints what changes may be necessary or what conceptions must be modified, but to make those changes you must act. You must take actions.

ACTION

A character in a drama is defined by the actions he takes and his methods in taking them. The more carefully he chooses his actions, the more chance he will have for success. If he chooses improper actions, or takes no action, he will have little impact on the resolution of the drama. Similarily, the less you do, or the more wrong choices you make, the less control you will have over your own life.

What exactly is an action? What is a right action? Suppose, for example, you have a need, or desire, that only one other person can fulfill. You go to see this person. The way you approach the problem will ultimately determine how much cooperation you will receive. Among the different actions you might attempt are to:

charm	contest	irritate
challenge	encourage	provoke
demand	inspire	conquer
plead	shame	delay
implore	embarrass	compromise
protest	scold	placate
beg	humor	cajole
accost	tease	patronize
confront	humiliate	beguile
command	vilify	devastate
dominate	criticize	impress
subdue	oppose	mystify
titilate	rouse	bewitch
tantalize	quash	intrigue
torment	inflame	terrify
urge	assault	threaten
incite	surmount	please
induce	bait	dazzle
intimidate	excite	deflate
allure	alarm	inflate
pacify	hassle	defy
flatter	goad	harass

In fact, there are more than two thousand verbs in the English language. More than two thousand different possible actions you can take at any time. Some of them will prove effective, others will cause you to fail.

As children, we utilize a vast number of verbs. We run. Hit. Scream. Fight. Argue. Bait. Tease. Complain. Push. And, most important, play. But the verbs we use as adults are fewer, and different. We work. Talk. Watch. Think. Worry. And, still, complain. "Play" is usually limited to planned leisure time activities. We "play" cards. By the time we are adults, most of us have lost the ability to "play," to act spontaneously, to act without prior thought or consideration. That sense of freedom to play we loved as children has disappeared. Parents, forced maturity, and structured schooling all work to impose a sense of reality and an understanding of responsibility. We are taught that certain behavior is expected at a certain time and anything different from that is wrong. Spontaneity is cut off. Instead of having access to two thousand different choices, we become limited to perhaps fifty socially acceptable actions.

Reading this book without beginning to take specific actions toward making changes in your life would be like trying to learn how to swim by simply reading an instructional booklet. It won't work. To swim you have to experience the texture of the water, you have to deal with your fears, and you must put into practice those techniques explained in the booklet. This book is about changing your life. To change you must take actions.

Rip this page out of the book.

Don't think about it. Tear this page out. Do it now.

Wherever you are, whatever you're doing, grip this page at the top, between your thumb and forefinger, and tear it free.

Enjoy it. It is permissible to rip this page out of this book. You are allowed to do it.

Were you able to do it? After the first command? The second? The third? After being given permission?

Children get great joy from tearing books apart, but as soon as they are old enough to understand, they are taught that books are to be read, not ripped. They are taught what is considered to be responsible social behavior. For better or worse, all the natural spontaneity, all the childhood joy of unrestricted play, is replaced by an arbitrary set of social values. So now, even when ordered, then asked, to tear a page out of a book, most people do not feel free enough to do it. They have learned from experience that conditions are attached to that action. Tearing the page will destroy the book. The book costs money. Or the book belongs to a friend who will become angry, or a library which will extract a penalty. Or they fear that someone might see them tearing the book and think them irresponsible.

This has been your second exercise. It makes absolutely no difference whether you actually tore the page out of the book or not. This is not a test and there is no right or wrong. The purpose of this exercise is to make you aware that much of your behavior is programmed by your upbringing and sense of social responsibility.

You were asked to play, to act spontaneously or "move freely within prescribed limits." Tearing a page out of a book is an action. You should see it as symbolic of the hundreds of other actions you have arbitrarily eliminated.

This is page 27. Except for this paragraph, it is almost a duplicate of the original page 27. But on that page the reader was told to rip the page out of the book, without thinking, wherever they were. It was an example of a spontaneous action. If page 27 is gone, please do not rip out this page. It's the last page 27 there is.

Children get great joy from tearing books apart, but as soon as they are old enough to understand, they are taught that books are to be read, not ripped. They are taught what is considered to be responsible social behavior. For better or worse, all the natural spontaneity, all the childhood joy of unrestricted play, is replaced by an arbitrary set of social values. So now, even when ordered, then asked, to tear a page out of a book, most people do not feel free enough to do it. They have learned from experience that conditions are attached to actions. Tearing the page will destroy the book. The book costs money. Or the book belongs to a friend who will become angry or a library which will extract a penalty. Or they fear that someone might see them tearing the book and think them irresponsible.

Considering whether or not to tear the page out of the book is the second exercise. It makes absolutely no difference whether the page is torn or not. This is not a test and there is no right or wrong. The purpose of this exercise is to make you aware that much of your behavior is programmed by your upbringing and sense of social responsibility.

You were asked to play, to act spontaneously or "move freely within prescribed limits." Tearing a page out of a book is an action. You should see it as symbolic of the hundreds of other actions you have arbitrarily eliminated from your life.

CONDITION

How you *felt* about being asked to shatter this rule of responsibility is called your condition. Some people might have been shocked by the order. Others might have found it mildly amusing, and still others completely pleasurable. Shock, amusement, and pleasure are feelings. When you were a child, every action you took was a result of feelings. You wanted something, you reached out for it. You did not want something, you pushed it away. As you matured, the actions triggered by feelings acquired greater meanings. You did not want something, you pushed it away, and suddenly you felt guilty for hurting someone's feelings.

The particular feeling you experience at a given moment is your condition. It is the way you feel inside.

Remember what you felt when you read the command to tear page 27 out of this book. Try, for a moment, to bring the same awareness you brought to your breathing to those feelings. Understanding your condition is the beginning of becoming aware of your "character." Other people, when asked to take exactly the same action, have totally different feelings, or they conceal or reveal them differently. Their "character," the role they play in life, is different.

Awareness of your condition is absolutely necessary if you seriously want to make changes in your life. Before you can change your condition, you must become aware of what it is.

PLACE

The way you responded to the second exercise is a means to examine your condition. Did you feel free to take that action? If you had been told a duplicate page followed and you would not be harming the book by tearing it, would your action have been the same? Would you have responded the same way if you had been in a different place, for example in a crowded subway car or in the reading room of a library? Would you have taken the same action if your parent or partner had been sitting with you? Would you have felt differently if it had been earlier or later in the day? The answers to those questions should provide you with information about yourself. You may discover that you are more limited in your actions than you believed. Remember how you responded to this exercise as you read this book.

OBJECTIVE

There are also exercises in this book designed to enable you to take actions to make changes, but what will those changes be? The madcap French detective created by Peter Sellers, Inspector Clouseau, is constantly taking actions, but inevitably they are the wrong actions taken at the wrong time. Action without specific purpose is aimless. Actions an actor takes on stage are planned and rehearsed beforehand. The actor knows what he is trying to accomplish with every action. In exactly the same way, you should know what your goals are before deciding what actions to take. You must have an objective.

You will accomplish little by freeing yourself to take new actions unless you know precisely what you are trying to accomplish. Do you intend to revitalize a dull relationship? Or free yourself from the control of another person? Or discover a worthwhile way of spending your time? Or rid yourself of constant tension? Perhaps even shatter the trap you find yourself in. Whatever your intention is, you must be aware of it before choosing the proper actions to take.

Most actors break a script into small chunks when preparing a characterization. They analyze the dialogue by "beats," or changes in intention. They decide exactly what the character is trying to accomplish. Is the character trying to charm someone? Dominate them? Gain sympathy? Frighten? Cajole? By understanding the intention, they can choose the proper action to perform. Few people take the time to determine their own intentions, to "block out" the script of their life. Having the tools is not enough. A sculptor would not begin chipping away aimlessly at a slab of marble in hopes that he might somehow end up with a magnificent piece of art. You must know precisely what you want to end up with, your aim, before you begin taking actions.

Actions may change as you select your goals. As you can change your role in a play or get up in the morning and change your costume, you can choose a new intention. Acting is a wonderful medium for growth because it allows you the opportunity to practice using different intentions in simulated situations. It allows you to rehearse for life. Working with a scene from a play or an improvisation from your own life, you can actually try out different solutions to a problem. You will ultimately reject many of the potential solutions as wrong, inappropriate, or useless, but there is no penalty attached to making attempts. Your goal is to achieve your aims. To do that you first become aware of your condition and your capabilities. Then you choose the objective, learn how to become emotionally free to take any of the great range of possible actions, prepare to take the most complete actions, and finally act to fulfill your needs and desires.

Being an actor—a person who can take a wide range of actions—qualifies you to become anything your imagination can project. You can become the leading player, the star, of the longest running show in town.

CHAPTER TWO:
Get Your Act Together

Our remedies oft in ourselves do lie,
Which we ascribe to Heaven.

—SHAKESPEARE

The greatest performance I ever gave had nothing to do with the theatre. For two years I created and lived the life of another person. The role was always challenging, constantly changing. It required me to make countless instant decisions, to choose between options, to select specific actions and carry out each one completely and convincingly. I had to create a totally believable character, and live my life as that character, all day, every day. Much of the material in this book is based on discoveries I made during that period.

I was drafted in 1956. After finishing Army basic training I was shipped to Fort Lewis, Washington, for eventual delivery to Korea. During normal troop processing I arrived at the desk of a second lieutenant who carefully examined my forms. Noticing my name and my college, the University of Texas, he asked, "You ever play pro football?"

I had broken my collarbone playing football during my sophomore year at Archer City High. Other than that, the closest I'd been to a football field was Row 28, Section E, in the Cotton Bowl bleachers. "No," I said.

He seemed surprised at my answer. "Oh," he said, sounding just a little disappointed, "Just college ball, eh?" Without waiting for my answer, he stood up, grabbed my forms, and walked into the commander's office.

Thus began my long-running role. Eventually, I would write an article about it for *Sports Illustrated* and *Reader's Digest* and discuss it on national television with Johnny Carson. But at that moment I was very scared. The lieutenant hurried back to his desk with a smile on his face—a rare sight for a private—and said, "Soldier, report for immediate flight to Japan."

At nine o'clock the next morning I was flying to Japan. On the flight were twenty-six officers, a 6'4", 225 pound, All-American football player from Notre Dame named Art Hunter, and I. Hunter sat next to me and said very little outside of, "To hell with the Army" and "It's colder 'n hell up here." Fortunately he didn't mention football. The only thing I knew for certain about football was that I didn't play it.

When we arrived at Haneda Air Base outside Tokyo, a corporal was waiting with a black military sedan. We drove directly to Camp Zama, United States Army Forces Far East, and stopped directly in front of the commanding officer's headquarters. The corporal led us directly to the man himself.

He sat behind a big desk, a stern-looking, cigar-smoking colonel. "Boys," he said to Hunter and me, "it's good to have you with us. The big game with Navy is next week. We intend—no, we *are* going to win it." He looked Hunter up and down like a rancher judging a prize bull and said, "You look in great shape, boy." Then he turned to me and hesitated a moment with a look of concern. He broke it with a smile and, "Must be pretty fast, eh?"

The colonel explained that he was a football supporter of no small repute. "We had that lieutenant assigned to Fort Lewis just to see we get the very best athletes over here. We already have Larry Hartshorn from the Cardinals and Mike Takacs, who played with the Packers."

None of this explained why they had me. That came later.

The colonel instructed the corporal to drive to his pet project, the new post football field. Thirty or forty of the biggest giants I have ever seen were at one end of the field doing little things like knocking the hell out of one another with paralyzing lunges. By now I was experiencing a fear and internal weakness few men have known and I was trying to emulate the attitude and gait of my All-American companion, who would just be another one of the boys to this crowd.

The coach halted the activity long enough for our introduction. I shook hands personally with each member of the team. Since I was already shaking all over, all I had to do was hold my hand out.

The next step was the football barracks, reserved exclusively for the football players, with Japanese houseboys to make up the beds, shine the shoes, care for the laundry, and do the housekeeping. For this it might be worth risking a few broken bones.

I was just beginning to relax when I heard a noise like the mob scenes in a Cecil B. De Mille spectacular. The gladiators were returning. I lay on my bunk feigning sleep. When my two roommates started talking, I finally learned the truth. I was being confused with a halfback named George Robinson from the University of Texas. The fact that my name was Robertson, Warren, seemed not to make a bit of difference. I was here, so I had to be a football player, and I was "Robbie" from here on in.

I shall never forget putting on the football pads and uniform for that first practice. The shoes were the only thing I was sure of. I watched the man suiting up next to me with all the concentrated attention of a first-year medical student attending a demonstration in anatomy. As I started jogging toward the practice field, I was sure something would drop off any minute.

Once on the field, I just kept running around and around it. "Laps " they call them. I was afraid to stop. I had to exercise utmost restraint to keep from running right on across the street, out the gate, and down the road. Every time I ran by the coach, I panted the words, "Gettin' in shape, gettin' in shape." He must have thought I was one devoted athlete, because I set a record for laps around a football field.

By practice the next morning, I was almost ready to confess the Army's error and plead insanity. At the completion of calisthenics, the coach called out various players' names for the starting team. I got a green shirt, symbolic of being a starter. So here I was, huddled with a group of what seemed to me the largest men ever assembled, preparing to oppose a team of the second-largest men ever assembled. The honor of carrying the ball first was awarded to none other than the newly arrived player—me! The only thing I was certain of about carrying a football was that I shouldn't be doing it.

So, with what voice I could find to speak, I requested that I just run straight ahead and asked if the quarterback would be so kind as to hand me the ball gently. When the ball was snapped to the quarterback, I just aimed at Art Hunter's back, shut my eyes, and ran. About three feet forward I felt something slap me in the pit of my stomach. I grabbed my midsection and, to my amazement, I was locked around the football still going forward. I must have run eight or ten yards before I fell headlong over a prone body on the ground.

That was the longest distance I had ever run with my eyes closed.

When I returned to our huddle, the backslaps from my teammates were almost enough to exhaust the little energy I had left. Because I had done so well the first time, the quarterback called my number again. This time I mustered up the courage to try it with my eyes open. Big Art Hunter opened a hole so big even my grandmother could have made a ten-yard run through. But, just the same, when we returned to the huddle the backslaps were for me.

The rest of the afternoon when I stumbled, fumbled, or goofed, everyone marked it up to my being out of shape or my unique style. They just wouldn't allow me to be less than the player they thought I was.

The big game with Navy was two days later. As we sat in the locker room, all dressed in our brand-new playing uniforms, I was petrified with fright. The coach and post commander gave us a pep talk. The band was playing. Nearly two thousand eager fans were cheering. There was something almost hypnotic about the atmosphere. Maybe I was going crazy, but I was beginning to believe I really was a football player.

I had a chance to prove it almost immediately. Navy kicked off. Maybe they knew something, they kicked right at me. All I could think of was, "Don't drop it, don't drop it; hug it, but don't drop it." When I caught it and started moving forward, it was the progress of a man mad with fear, and no madman ever moved faster. Later the coach made some remark about it being the fastest movement for a short distance he had ever witnessed.

The rest of the game I was in some kind of trance. I did everything a man would do for survival. And, for me, that's just what it was. When the game ended, I was one of the leading ground gainers, having used only my favorite straight-ahead play. My maniacal rompings had scored one touchdown and assisted with another.

As the football season progressed, my fear of being discovered as counterfeit lessened. I watched how the real players acted and tried to copy them. I spent many nights at the post library learning football terms and strategy. And it all worked. I spent two football seasons playing for Camp Zama as a regular starter, and the team was good enough to win the conference championship. Sometimes, when I think back on it, the whole adventure seems impossible. But it happened. I spent two years as another character, and I have the scrapbooks to prove it.

Obviously, I couldn't have survived without some natural athletic ability, but the real reason my characterization was successful was the attention I paid to my actions. I acted the role of a football player. I had one clear-cut intention: don't get caught. With that always in mind, I chose specific actions to help me achieve that objective. At night I would lie on my bunk, reassess the day, and try to plan my actions for the following day. I broke the day into smaller parts, as an actor breaks a script into parts, and considered all the options available to me. From those options I selected the proper actions. Eventually, I didn't need this exercise. I began to think as a football player, gained confidence in myself as a football player, and even began to believe I was a football player. The proper actions came naturally.

In fact, I actually became a good football player. The significant aspect of the story is that, all the time, for two years, this football player was really me. The hard-hitting running back was simply an aspect of myself I had never explored. I didn't realize that while at Camp Zama; I thought I was playing a role, but it was real life. I was never anyone else. My character was me. It was my own perception of my abilities that caused me to believe I was playing the part of a fictional character I'd been forced to create.

You, too, have potential you've never explored. Your ideas of what is possible for yourself, ideas often formed during childhood and never again examined or updated, limit you and prevent you from taking actions to change. It is possible to change your life role, as I proved at Camp Zama, even if you don't have Art Hunter blocking for you. Grandma Moses, for example, didn't even *start* painting until she was seventy-six years old. Unlike the stage, where an author provides words for his characters, in life we have the right to change the script. There is no authority in the world that can punish you for initiating change, for trying to improve your life, as long as your actions don't infringe on the liberties of others. You may not be taking advantage of that right because you've forgotten it exists. You've been following the same script the same way for so long, you may have come to believe change is not possible.

The way to change your life is to start taking new actions. Actions create change in your environment, in the way other people see you, in the way you see yourself. I discovered a long time ago there is no such thing as a person being a success or a failure. There are only people who take actions that fail or succeed. Life is nothing more than a progression of actions against obstacles. If you select the right actions, you will overcome the obstacles. If you try to overcome the obstacles with the wrong actions, you will fail.

You may be among the many people who are unhappy because they can't seem to make contact with others, for example. Perhaps you're too shy, or overly aggressive, or simply don't know how to attract other people. You try, but nothing works. Obviously, you are doing something wrong—no matter how well dressed you are, or how confident you feel, whatever actions you are taking, are the wrong actions. Every action may not be wrong, but at least enough are to make you ineffective. You are not reaching the goal you set for yourself; therefore your actions are wrong.

In this case, each action must be individually examined and many of them must be replaced. Are you too confident? Are you overdressed for a casual place? Do you sit in a corner and wait for people to come to you? Is the type of place you've selected right for the type of person you want to meet? Do you have any idea what you will say in the beginning of a conversation? In later chapters we will be examining the importance of each of these factors in your life, to help you select actions that might work for you. But whatever actions you finally select, you must begin by eliminating those you are now taking. You're not meeting people, they are not working for you. No matter how secure you feel in taking them, no matter how much you identify these actions as "the real me," they are wrong and should be replaced.

WHAT IS AN ACTION?

An action is what we do to satisfy our needs and desires. A single action is a step toward reaching an objective, while a string of actions, taken correctly, enable you to achieve your objective. Although we tend to think of action as movement, it is not necessarily so. Remaining still when ordered to "come here" is an action of challenge, defiance, or even obstinacy.

RIGHT ACTION

What is the right action? It is simply the action that gets you what you need or desire. The one that makes happen what you want to happen. The one that helps you overcome an obstacle. The one that enables you to reach an objective. If you are starving, the right action puts food in your mouth. If you are lonely, it is the one that provides companionship. The right action is the one that works.

NEEDS AND DESIRES

Finding that action, or series of actions, requires that you first determine exactly what it is you need or desire. What do you want? What is your overall objective? At Camp Zama, I did not want to be uncovered as an imposter. Knowing that, I could be consistent in my actions. Every action I took helped me achieve that objective. Your objective may be getting a better job, or a raise. Improving your home life. Meeting new people. Recovering from a disastrous relationship. Losing weight. Overcoming constant depression. It may be something as simple as cutting back on the hours spent in front of your television set, or as complicated as changing your entire lifestyle.

Often these needs and desires get very complicated. It is important to sort out the difference between the two. By fulfilling your needs, you create a situation in which achieving your desires is possible, but you must know the difference.

Needs are the basic essentials necessary for well-being. A healthy body. Food. Shelter. Peace of mind. Another person. These are the basics for life. A sleek car is not essential to happiness. A vacation retreat is not essential to contentment. A trip to Europe is not necessary for enjoyment. Because we live in world where dreams are really possible, it is easy to forget that they are not really necessary for happiness. When Elia Kazan cast James Dean into *East of Eden*, he asked the young actor to fly to California with him so they could go over the script. Dean, a virtually unknown Broadway actor at this point, carried all his possessions in a cardboard box. Kazan realized that Dean had no money and gave him a five hundred dollar advance on his paycheck.

Before dawn the following morning, Kazan arrived on the set to do some preproduction thinking. Although it was far too early for anyone else to be on the set, in the distance he thought he saw a horse. As he walked closer, he saw it was indeed a horse, and a man standing with it, rubbing its neck. Finally he saw it was James Dean. Kazan asked him what he was doing on the set at dawn with a horse.

Dean answered, "All my life I said if I ever made enough money, the one thing I wanted was a horse. So I bought one." He had taken his five hundred dollar advance and purchased this horse.He had fulfilled a strong need. This horse made his life satisfying. It made him content. For him, it was a necessity. He might have desired a whole stable of horses, but he truly needed this one horse.

Each person has very personal needs and desires. What you may truly need to make your life complete may just be an accessory for someone else. Your needs may be another person's desires. Some people really need a partner in life. Others may be quite happy and content alone, although they desire the company of another person.

On a separate piece of paper make two columns. Title one column *"Needs,"* and the other *"Desires."* Then list what you really need, and really desire. The needs should be absolutely truthful, the desires absolutely unfettered, no matter how extravagant, how extraordinary, how fantastic. You may find this list difficult. Is a color television set essential? Will it fulfill one of your basic needs? If so, put it on your list as a need. But if it is a luxury item, something you desire, put it in that column. Once you have begun this vitally important list, hang it up where you will see it and be able to add to and subtract from it as you change your mind.

Eventually this will be your list of objectives. You will know what it is you really want. You will know what you want to gain from this book. And you will be able to set goals.

Once you have made this list and defined your own objectives, you next must begin to determine what actions to take. Start by considering the entire scope of possible actions. These are actions not limited by time, distance, morality, legal considerations, or economic factors. These are actions you can really take. Other actions can be eliminated because they are obviously the wrong ones. Actions should be selected to emphasize your strengths and play down your weaknesses. They should be strong enough to overcome the competing actions of other people. And they should take the environment into consideration. Every action must directly contribute toward accomplishing your overall objective.

The more clearly and concisely you define that objective, the easier it will be to select only the actions which will help you achieve it. Work at your list until you are really satisfied that it includes those things that you really believe will make you satisfied and happy. Although choosing specific actions to reach these objectives might sound limiting, it is one of the most liberating things you can do. By knowing precisely what it is you are trying to accomplish at a given moment, and understanding how you intend to accomplish it, in life or on stage, it is possible to bring your complete attention, every tool you have at your disposal, to that moment.

Too often people dissipate their energies trying to achieve great, undefined goals instead of focusing on a single objective. In the same way you learned to focus your complete attention on your breath, you can bring your entire awareness to a single action. The important thing is remembering your objective. Once you are sure of that, everything else will fall into place.

One evening, during the performance of an Off-Broadway show, the leading male actor forgot his lines. The scene was taking place in a handsomely decorated living room and he was alone with a beautiful woman. His objective, we learned earlier in the play, was to seduce her. To accomplish this feat, he had chosen to overwhelm her with sophistication. He was charming and witty and debonair. Suddenly, he forgot his lines. Instead, he concentrated on his objective and chosen actions. "Excuse me, only for a moment," he said charmingly. "Let me go to my library. There is a book I'd love to show you." A moment later he returned with the book—the stage manager's bound copy of the script—and read his lines. Because this actor had a clear understanding of his objective and actions, he was able to recover gracefully. Other actors in the same situation wouldn't even have left the stage. By remembering the actions they chose, they would either recall the line or ad-lib sufficiently to get through the scene.

Your objective might be to get a raise. There are many different actions possible. You can go into the manager's office and implore. Or you can barge in and demand it. Or walk in gently and plead. Or threaten to quit. Or badger him over a period of time. Or, to gain sympathy, tell him that your rent is overdue and your children are sick. Or tell him a joke to entertain him. Or try all of these. Or some. Or choose from numerous other possibilities. Some of these actions will help you get your raise; others will not. By learning as much as possible about the manager, about the situation, and about the environment, you can plan your actions and vastly increase your chances for success.

There is a reason you selected specific actions. You thought they would work. The more information you have about the circumstances, the easier it will be to select proper actions.

Once you have selected those actions you believe will work, it should be a simple matter of just carrying them out. Unfortunately, that simple matter is not at all simple. You go through life utilizing a very limited number of actions. You know what it is you want. You may even be able to select those actions which will prove successful, yet you are not capable of carrying them out. You know that if you demand a raise, the manager will give it to you. Yet you are incapable of demanding, or threatening, or pleading. You have lost the use of many important actions. You have lost the freedom to act.

From the moment we are born, people start depriving us of our actions. Children have a built-in mechanism for action. They explore everything. They touch, smell, listen, and if something is small enough, even swallow it. They explore their bodies with the same innocent interest as they would explore a rubber ball. To a child, this sensory exploration and an action are exactly the same thing. Every part of the child is concentrating on the exploration of whatever is in front of him. His mind, body, and emotions, uncluttered, are all focusing on this single action, and this action is totally complete.

At this stage of development, there is no reasoning process. There are no mental obstructions. A child wants; he reaches out and takes. The mind is a clear slate, the senses not yet departmentalized. The weather, for example, does not yet have a separate identity. It is not good, not bad; it just is.

Over a period of time experience begins to record impressions. Rain has a sound. A feel. And even before the child understands words, a sense memory commences.

Then, as words take on meanings, thoughts are imprinted on that clean slate. Although some of them may be those of the child, most often these thoughts are those of authority figures, usually parents. Since their ability to take action is stronger than the child's, their thoughts and beliefs impose the first limitations. "Don't touch that." "Don't play now." "Eat this, it's good for you, but don't eat too much." Their limitations become the child's.

Suddenly thoughts intrude between the impulse to act and the manifestation of the action. The child wants, but if he reaches out and takes, his hand will get slapped. Now taking an action involves a certain responsibility. Instead of just taking or pushing away or holding tightly, or waving, or hitting, the child must wonder what the result of the action will be. Will pushing a ball away result in punishment or disapproval? For survival, as children, we learn to suppress purely emotional impulses.

The result is that, as adults, we end up attaching complicated thoughts to what should be simple actions. The mind, knowing the penalties for taking wrong actions, simply represses all but the safest actions. In this way, we believe, we will be loved, we will be given approval, and our lives will be better and safer. It makes no difference that the people who deprived us of our actions, the people who originally limited us, no longer have that power. The mind has learned to not allow risks to be taken.

The inability to take actions is a handicap. Life is less than it might be. But, for an actor, it can be devastating. I had one student who could not smile. His lips stayed clasped together, and when he wanted to show some sort of happy reaction he would cautiously raise the corners of his mouth. Obviously, this was going to make it impossible for him to play almost anything but somber roles. Even off-stage, he simply never smiled, so I assumed he had bad teeth and was afraid to show them. Finally, by gaining his trust, and using some very bad jokes, I cajoled him to open his mouth and smile broadly. He had great teeth. He even had an appealing smile. Later, I discovered he did not smile because he thought he was ugly when he smiled. His mother told him that repeatedly when he was a child, and because he loved her, and believed her, he stopped smiling. He lost the ability to smile. Why did his mother do that? If I were to go into all the things that parents unknowingly do to their children, this would become a very different kind of book. Like most parents, she probably thought she was doing this for his own good, never realizing the consequences her actions would have.

Once he was aware of the problem, this actor easily overcame it. The ability to take every action we were once capable of taking is still inside all of us. In survival situations particularly, when there is no time to consider what actions are possible, people suddenly take actions out of the ordinary. A wealthy businessman, for example, was robbed and locked in the trunk of his car. He realized that he only had a limited amount of air, and instead of expending what little air there was by futilely trying to smash through the steel trunk, he unscrewed the cap on the spare tire and used the air in the tire to breathe until his wife discovered him. And it is not unusual to read about people performing great feats of strength to save the life of someone they love.

The crisis does not have to be a life-and-death matter; it can just as easily concern day-to-day survival. For me, in Japan, survival meant learning how to act like a football player, as well as learning how to play the game. For you, the bills can just get too high, the job too frustrating, the relationship too difficult. Finally, you will protest. Or, finally, you feel the need to hit back. Or, finally, you get up the courage to make demands. Given the right conditions, you are capable of exercising every possible action. Unfortunately, the right conditions may never happen, and you may remain stuck where you are. To help you take these actions, we use exercises.

The inability to take certain actions will prevent an actor from reaching his full potential as a performer. To help the actor regain the complete use of actions, we use exercises called personalizations.

PERSONALIZATIONS

Personalizations are rehearsals for life. They are exercises, a method of willfully practicing an action so it eventually becomes natural, whether it is to be performed on stage or used in real life. Personalizations enable individuals to take extremely difficult actions without any possibility of punishment or penalty. It allows them to test their actions in a friendly, controlled environment. It allows them to put desires into words and then into actions.

I had an attractive girl student who was not capable of giving a command. No matter how hard she tried, every command sounded like a request. I asked her to make a personalization, to imagine that the person who first prevented her from giving commands was standing in front of her. I helped her create an image of this other person. Then I told her to command that person to leave the room.

She grimaced, pointed at the door, and said in a meek voice, "Get out of this room. Please?"

I asked her to be a bit more commanding.

"I would like you to leave this room right now. All right?"

Then, "Leave this room, okay?" By this point even she was laughing at her inability to take this seemingly simple action.

She tried again. "Could you please leave this room?"

And again. "Would you mind leaving the room?"

I am in no way exaggerating. This totally mature woman must have attempted ten different ways of giving a simple command. To take the action of commanding. But she was absolutely unable to do it. Somewhere, at some time in her life, she had been robbed of the ability to take that action. She was not capable of commanding anyone to do anything. She no longer knew the proper tone to use, the correct posture, she didn't even know the right words.

I explained this to her and gave her the correct words to repeat, "Get out of this room and do it now!" I gave her the tone, a gruff, no-nonsense tone, and she repeated it. Then she repeated it again. I reminded her that she was speaking directly to the person who had not allowed her to be commanding. She was finally standing up to that person. She repeated it once more, "Get out of this room and do it now," in a firm voice. Once she gave that simple command and saw that no penalties were involved—the sky did not fall, no one had stopped loving her—she began to recover the ability to make commands.

Personalizations are extremely important exercises. These "rehearsals for life" will enable you to do things you were previously unable to do. In a way, they allow you to create a "crisis" situation in a completely controlled environment. They allow you to see what you are capable of, without any risks. Besides that, they are easy, and fun.

Take a chair and stand a few feet away, directly in front of it. Now think of a person who has been particularly important in your life. This person may have been the most benevolent, helpful, and loving person you've ever known, but, strangely enough, they may also have been the most damaging to your ability to carry out a wide range of actions. Most often this person is a parent, although it doesn't have to be.

Imagine that person is sitting in the chair in front of you. The composite parts of the imagination to use are sight, sound, and smell. Use your senses to remember as much as you can about that person. Remember the color of their hair and the way they combed it. Remember the way they looked at you. Remember their attitude, the style of the clothes they wore. The scent of their cologne, or perfume, or hair spray. Remember the sound of their voice. Let your imagination be free to "see" that person. This is a sense memory.

Remember, you are not going to hurt anybody, nor will you be hurt. No damage will be done to anyone. This is just an exercise, a practice session. Consider it a type of "play." The person is not really in the chair. They might not even be alive anymore. Don't try to protect that person, nothing can happen to them. The object of this exercise is to relearn, and rehearse, an action.

Now, select an action you were never allowed to take with that person. Speak to that person. Out loud. Allow yourself to feel your shyness or embarrassment. Confront this person. Or demand something. Tell them, "I want . . . " Challenge them. Ask for something. Criticize. Tell this person off as you were never permitted to. Protest about the way you were treated. It makes no difference which action you select. It might be one of these or any other you choose. This person can't punish you. You won't be hit. You won't be deprived of food. You won't be deprived of love.

Use your body for emphasis. Strike out with your hands. Allow your body to speak freely to the person in the chair. Let your hands articulate. Let whatever physical movements that occur naturally just happen; don't stop any movement at all.

Whatever action you choose, the words should fulfill it. Sometimes, because you don't know how to take the action, you won't know the right words. The particular words are not important. Eventually the right ones will come. Try to use your own words but, if they don't come naturally, if you have to stop and think about what you're saying, substitute numbers. Confront this person by counting from one to ten. Demand in the same voice, the same tone you would use if you had the words, but substitute numbers. It is the taking of the action, not the particular words, that is important. Once you've experienced this, you'll find your own words.

As an alternative to using numbers, we often use monologues from plays. The particular monologue makes no difference. It is to be used for practice, just as a pianist uses sheet music. Personalizations allow you to run scales on your body, but instead of notes, you use words. At the end of this book are a series of selected monologues. If you feel the need to use words other than your own, turn to the back of the book and use the monologues.

Personalizations are the foundation of my work. Students learn how to make a personalization in class, and then make them on their own whenever they feel it necessary. Throughout this book I've included excerpts from classroom exercises. The purpose of this is to show you how the exercises are conducted in class, as well as to convey the information that comes from them.

The following personalization exercise was done by a

male student who had difficulty expressing any emotion:

The student was seated in a comfortable chair on a stage in front of the room.

WARREN: Are you comfortable?

STUDENT: Yes. Thanks.

WARREN: Now, try to remember a time when you wept out of fear or pain or anger. Remember the last time you revealed emotion to yourself. Don't tell me the narrative, just describe it to me sensorily, the things that come into your mind. The colors, the sound, whatever you remember.

STUDENT: I can just remember one occasion. I'm in a room. There's a desk. The door is on the righthand side. A lot of papers are on the desk. I'm sitting near the door. The venetian blinds are drawn. The closet is near me. There's a chest, it's mahogany, with about twenty drawers in it. The floor tiles are red and brown, with little streaks of white in them.

WARREN: Please go to the feeling now.

STUDENT: I don't really remember. I'm not exactly sure . . .

WARREN: I want you to say all the things you wanted to say, whether you said them at that time or not. I want you to say them all now, right now.

STUDENT: *(His voice starting to rise as he personalizes)* That's not what I expected of you. What do you think you're trying to prove, huh? You gotta be out of your mind, you know that? You think I'm going to trust you after that? You think so? You really got to be out of your mind.

WARREN: Find the words, please.

STUDENT: *(Getting angry now)* Look! I don't care what you do anymore. I trusted you, and as far as I'm concerned, you're not worth it. I don't give a damn what you think anymore, you hear what I'm saying, I don't care. I don't want to see it your way. It doesn't make any sense to me.

WARREN: Tell them how they hurt you. Criticize.

STUDENT: *(Starting to yell)* You did a really lousy thing, you know. That was rotten. You hurt me. You didn't have to hurt me. That was stupid. You're stupid. You know that, you're stupid. I hate you for that. I hate you.

WARREN: Use your body to show them that feeling, please. Don't be afraid to strike out with your hands. Confront them.

STUDENT: *(Thrusting out both hands in front of him the full length of his arms)* I said I hate you. You hear me? You hear what I said. I hate you. I hate you. I hate you.*(He starts crying as he thrusts out his arms)* You bitch. I hate you. You hurt me.

WARREN: Now tell them what you really want. Appeal.

STUDENT: Why did you hurt me? I never did anything to you. I never asked you for anything. I just . . . I just . . . wanted you to love me. That's all. I hate you. I hate you so much. I never want to see you again.

WARREN: Please tell this person what you really want. Tell them you want them to love you. Implore.

STUDENT: *(Breathing very deeply. His anger subsides into tears)* Please love me. Please. Please. I want you to love me so bad. Please hold me. Please. Please. Please. *(He continues crying).*

WARREN: Would you relax for a moment, please. Take a drink of water, please. *(Waits until the student regains his composure.)* Only you know what happened in your youth, but you seem buried under granite. When we first started working it was impossible to get any emotion out of you, but now, now, when you start to smile, you really project warmth. When I use the word weep, your mind probably thinks I'm crazy. Cry? It doesn't know what I'm talking about. But your feelings know exactly what I'm saying. You've buried your feelings very deeply; now we have to excavate them. You have to relearn that it is permissible to show your real feelings, that you can handle your emotions now.

You're thawing out, you know that, don't you? Your body had become deadened to feeling. Nature equips some animals with shells, You have a shell, too. Just like any other shell, it is a kind of protection. Now, for the first time, your shell is getting softer, it's starting to let go. You're starting to feel again.*(Listening to this, tears filled the eyes of the student and he started to brush them away.)*

Let the feeling go, please. Don't stop what you're feeling. Continue to breathe evenly, please. Don't stop the feeling. *(The student weeps for a few minutes, then stops and breathes deeply.)* How do you feel, now?

STUDENT: Good, I feel very good. I feel like I'm about six years old.

WARREN: Is that good?

STUDENT: Yeah, I like that.

Your personalization will probably not be as dramatic as this student's, at least not at first. But allow yourself to become completely involved in it and you'll find real feeling welling up inside you. Let the feeling come to the surface. Do not stop it. Just feel it.

After completing your first personalization, using your own words, numbers, one of the monologues at the back of the book, or a monologue of your own choosing, try it again. This time, change your actions as you go through it. Start by demanding, or pleading, or whatever you choose, and switch to a second and then a third action during the personalization. Try to open your mouth completely and speak firmly, and use your body for punctuation.

Once you feel secure doing a personalization, it is permissible to have a real person, someone you trust, sitting in the chair in front of you. Allow that person to become a stand-in for the authority figure. You should still be speaking to that imaginary individual—personalizing—and all your actions should be directed at that person. At first your partner should be silent. Later, when you're comfortable speaking to another figure, he can actually take the role of the authority figure, and respond with opposing actions.

These exercises should not last long. They may be repeated as often as you desire. The more often you practice, the better able you will be to take action. Many students find their bodies come alive with feeling after a personalization—their arms tingle, their heads feel light, sensations caused by long frozen emotions beginning to thaw.

Personalizations enable you to confront someone else in a way you have never been able to before. They teach you how to put actions into words and movements, and how to take actions at times and in situations in which you are normally unable to act. Hearing words you've held inside finally spoken is a great release—and it enables you to use those words in real situations. A close friend of mine had the unenviable job of firing an employee of his, and was unable to do it. He simply could not get the words out. He is not a student of mine and has never studied acting, so I explained exactly what a personalization was and how it was done. Then, sitting in his car, we did one; we rehearsed for life. I played the employee and argued with him as firmly as I could. I did not make it easy for him, but since he was aware that no penalties were involved he wouldn't feel guilty about firing me. He was able to do it. For him it was quite liberating. He heard his voice saying those things he'd been thinking and was afraid to say. Once he really got into it, he released a torrent of feelings about this worker whose part I was playing.

He called me the following day to tell me he'd fired the man and had no bad feelings about it at all. "He didn't do the job. There was really no reason I should have been afraid to fire him." But he was. By doing a personalization, by rehearsing this "terrible" act, he was able to fulfill an important responsibility.

Often, after their first few personalizations, my students will actually confront the person they imaginarily sat in the the chair, taking the precise actions they have been practicing. There is nothing wrong with that, but it is not the purpose of the exercise. Personalizations are not used to teach you how to get even with someone. Their purpose is to teach you how to take actions you are normally unable to take. Eventually you will be able to create personalizations about anyone you want to meet with a specific action, from attractive people to a troublesome coworker. With enough practice, the exercise will become unnecessary. You will have regained the ability to take all your desired actions.

It is unreasonable to believe that anyone can go through life selecting the proper action to use at every moment. But by using these exercises to regain the use of actions, by defining objectives and selecting specific actions, you can change your life. You can regain control of your life.

Once you have regained control of your own life and are not afraid to take an action for fear of hurting someone else, or risking your own security, the action-selection process will come naturally. You will begin doing what you want to do and you will feel that your actions are right. Your actions and reactions will become intuitive.

You will be free to act.

CHAPTER THREE:
Emotions—The Motive Power

In every cry of every man,
In every infant's cry of fear,
In every voice, in every ban,
The mind-forg'd manacles I hear.

—WILLIAM BLAKE

"I love you."

It can be said in a hundred different ways, or expressed in as many, or more. But love is not three little words, and it is not gifts; love is an emotion, a feeling. And if we were able to completely communicate that emotion, words wouldn't be necessary and gifts would have little meaning. Unfortunately, most people need the words and gifts to prove their love, since they cannot convey their true feelings.

Emotions are universal. Language is not. Knowledge is limited by access to information. Actions are dictated by local culture. But absolutely everybody is born with the ability to experience emotions, to feel. King Henry VIII, Robert

56

E. Lee, Babe Ruth, Ethel Merman, your mailman, and you all share the same feelings. Although triggered by different actions or circumstances, the basic emotions of love, anger, fear, rage, affection, sorrow, guilt, hate, anxiety, and contentment exist in all of us.

It is this universal understanding of emotions that makes it possible for writers and performers to place great themes in any setting and know the audience will relate to them. The sorrow the audience feels when the peasant Tevye is forced to leave his small Russian village of Anatevka in *Fiddler on the Roof* is exactly the same sorrow it feels when the depression forces the Joad family to abandon their Oklahoma dust bowl farmhouse in *The Grapes of Wrath*.

Emotions are the material for actions. The actions we take should be the attempt to satisfy them. In acting, the emotions or feelings of a character are called his "condition." The first thing a professional actor does when studying a script is determine the condition of the character he is to portray and how it changes progressively in the script. Once he has this knowledge, he can choose actions which will best express his character's condition.

It is not quite that simple in real life. Everyone has the innate ability to experience the full range of emotions, but few people do. Under certain conditions, in the safety of a dark theatre, or alone with someone you trust, for example, you allow yourself to feel and express emotions. But finding those same emotions in everyday life and taking actions based on them is difficult, sometimes impossible. You can satisfy all the physical needs and desires—eating when you "feel" hungry, taking medicine when you "feel" sick—but still manage to ignore the very real needs of the emotions.

Society almost demands it. We are trained not to show emotion in public. For the most part, we equate showing feelings in public with some sort of weakness, something to be embarrassed about.

As a substitute for taking actions based on real needs and

desires, instead of showing anger when we "feel" it, most adults offer a habitual social response. To get along with the rest of the world, to fit in, we feign feelings. Inside, we may be boiling with anger, but rather than risk disapproval by showing it, we try to smile and act pleasant. Only in a crisis situation—a time in which we respond instinctively rather than considering our actions—are real emotions allowed to surface. Otherwise we do our best to cope with these hidden emotions that are not permitted to be expressed.

Because we learn to hide these feelings so well, they are often lost and almost forgotten. The actions we take satisfy the needs and desires of the people around us, our supporting characters, rather than our own, and we are left with a vague feeling of being unfulfilled. Our life, our happiness, is controlled by others. We don't even know what it is we really want, because we've lost communications with the emotions which will tell us.

This process of trying to satisfy other people starts early in life. The human being can be broken down into numerous parts, but primary among them are the intellectual, emotional, and physical. We experience everything that happens to us on at least one of these levels. We think with our minds; we act and feel sensations with our bodies. As explained earlier, the first language is emotional. It prompts action without conscious thought. Long before we have the understanding to say, "I like you," we reach out and touch. Long before we have the proper words to demand, "I want," we take. Long before we can rationally decide, "Go away," we shove. There is an instant connection between our feelings and the actions we take, uninterrupted by the intellectual process.

Gradually, this primitive language of expression is replaced by comprehension of the spoken word and thought. For a brief time, a delicate balance exists between emotion and thought, and everything you experience is understood by the mind, but your reaction to it is based on your emotions. This is the ideal situation. The separate parts of your makeup are in harmony and you are a true "intellectual savage," able to understand precisely what your emotions demand and free to take the actions necessary to satisfy those needs. Unfortunately, this balance doesn't last very long.

Under normal circumstances your mind is in complete control of your body. It controls the switchboard that translates emotion into action. At first the intellect is benevolent, it allows the body to respond to the needs of the emotions. But eventually the mind learns that the result of this is often emotional pain or physical punishment. To prevent this, the mind gradually shuts off the emotions. Instead of routinely translating emotion into action, the mind protects the delicate emotions by ordering its own actions, actions which will not result in pain or punishment. So, rather than acting on what you feel, you end up acting on what you think, or imagine. All the wonderful excitement of spontaneous response disappears, replaced by intellectual behavior.

The result is often anxiety or tension, a feeling of wanting to do something, even needing to do something, but not being able to determine exactly what it is. Tension is caused by emotion without action. When you experience an emotion, the body summons up the energy to take the corresponding action that would reveal that emotion to the world. But when the action is repressed, when the mind does not allow the body to release that energy through action, it must go somewhere. The energy does not just disappear. It is stored in the muscles.

Eventually a great deal of energy exists in the muscles, energy that cannot be released. Like wood blocking a river, this energy prevents the muscles from moving freely and fluidly. The body becomes erect, the muscles tight with tension. That feeling of repressed energy is anxiety.

This condition often manifests itself in a high voice that is squeezed, or choked off at the throat, sweating, irregular breathing, stiff necks, bad backs, as well as nervous habits like grinding teeth at night, unconsciously shaking a foot, or even facial tics.

The way to rid yourself of this tension is to release the energy stored in your muscles. Physical exercise helps work some of it off, but unless you change your behavior, it simply collects again. The way to completely relax your body is to release this energy as it was originally intended to be released, through the expression of emotions. Initially, this can be done through personalization exercises. These exercises, during which you imaginarily recreate the situations which caused you to be tense and anxious, allow you to release all your pent-up emotions by acting out exactly what your emotions originally desired. You are free to explode with anger or burst out with derisive laughter, free to do exactly what your emotions command, and free from penalty.

The release of this anxiety-causing tension, at first through personalizations and later from the resulting changes in your behavior, will also result in physical changes. Back trouble, throat trouble, even sinus trouble may disappear. I've had students whose eyesight improved. With the relaxation of facial muscles, many students actually look younger. But, by far, the most striking change is weight loss. The body seems to store up weight as sort of a retainer for feeling. When the feeling starts to be released, the body actually vibrates and weight loss usually follows. Every overweight student I've ever had, without exception, has lost weight while studying with me.

What causes the body to store this energy rather than releasing it as emotion? Pain, mostly, and the desperate need to stop the hurt.

Emotional pain can result from many causes. One of the most difficult students I ever worked with was a handsome man in his early thirties. He had strong features and a muscular frame, but he was very meek. He was totally nonassertive, almost apologetic in his actions. For several months I tried to find those blocked feelings that caused him to be so apologetic, but I couldn't elicit any real feeling at all. I tried all the exercises I normally use in class; I tried to find some sense memory in his body, but nothing worked. Eventually, I had him hold his hands straight out. When he did this, his fingers moved as if they were touching something. I thought perhaps his emotions were remembering a photograph. That had happened before. A student's parents had died when she was very young and her only sense of physical feeling for them was to pick up a framed photograph and touch their images. She learned to equate the emotions for her parents with the feel of the glass in the picture frame. But this male student was not remembering a photograph. It was something more than that.

I knew it was a surface of some type, it had to be. "What are your hands feeling?" I asked.

"I'm not sure," he started. "No. I don't know. It's glass."

"A picture frame?"

He was insistent it was not a picture frame. "It's too cold." Eventually we discovered it was glass, but window glass. It was cold and it was dirty. He had to wipe his hands on his legs everytime he touched it. And it caused him great pain.

When he started feeling the pain, great anguish, the memories so deeply buried started coming back.

The first five years of his life had been spent in a German concentration camp. During that time he was separated from his parents. The only contact he had with them was watching as they exercised in the workyard, watching by pressing his hands and face against a cold, dirty pane of glass.

In the camp he learned not to show any emotion. The pain he felt was so intense his mind simply shut off all his feelings. It was better to feel nothing than to risk that incredible pain. So he grew up feeling nothing. Even when he was safe in the United States, his mind continued to protect his emotions, barricading the strong feelings he was terrified of showing behind a meek, docile exterior. Consciously, he had eliminated all memory of that camp, but subconsciously he had never allowed himself to forget.

In class, he began making personalizations which enabled him to act out the rage he was never permitted in that camp, to complete those feelings he had been holding inside almost his entire life. By finally allowing himself to expel that rage, learning not to feel guilty about it, and understanding he would no longer be punished for feeling, he reintroduced the entire range of emotions into his voice, body, and face. He literally became a new person.

Although few people experience anything so tragic so young, we all suffer childhood trauma and shut off some of our emotions. Little girls offer love to their fathers by climbing up on their legs, but many embarrassed fathers tell them not to, a response the child sees as rejection of their love. So they simply stop offering it. Little boys are scolded by their fathers for crying, for not "acting like a man." So they learn to do precisely that—act like a man, and lose the range of sensitive emotions. This happens because, as children, we equate our feelings with our value. Feelings are all we have to offer, and if they are not important, we are not important. Our feelings are not wanted; therefore we are not wanted. The result is emotional pain. We believe there is something wrong with us. We hurt. The mind has learned that to offer feelings openly is to risk pain. So, because they are a constant source of pain and embarrassment, we stop offering our feelings to the world to be abused. We have all been so deceived, betrayed, violated, and brutalized—often by people who love us and have only the very best intentions   that part of us simply withdraws. For our own protection, we allow the mind to take full control.

The goal of the mind is to protect the emotions. To survive. To insure there is no more pain. This often involves trying to please authority figures. Most authority figures try to limit action. Don't cry. Sit still. Act nice. Stop running. Don't move. Be quiet. Wait. Leave him alone. Put that down. Stay out of there. Keep your voice down. Don't touch that. Children lack the intelligence to distinguish between a conditon and an action. When they are ordered to stop an action, they also hide the feeling that initiated that action. Adults simply say to a child, "Stop kicking," rather than "Don't take an action with your anger," so we grow up believing a condition and an action are almost the same thing. If we are punished for taking an action, we believe we are being punished for the feeling as well. So we equate having a feeling with the punishment, never understanding it is possible to experience an emotion without taking a specific action to complete it. It is possible to feel, and express, sorrow without breaking down. It is possible to feel, and express, anger without having to punch somebody. By making the connection directly between emotion and punishment, the feeling is cut off.

Feelings remain isolated and unused because we have nothing in our educational system to train the emotions. We teach our brain to solve problems, we train our bodies to perform athletically, but the emotions receive only negative attention. They are taught what not to do.

For people in the theatre, gaining complete access to their emotions is the most important aspect of training. This is the first work I do with beginning students. If an actor cannot really experience his own feelings, then he certainly cannot invest a character with anything real. If he does not know how love "feels" and how it is naturally expressed, then his character cannot believably be in love.

I first learned the importance of bringing real emotion to acting while still at Camp Zama, in Japan. An American film company was in the country making the movie *Sayo-*

nara, starring Marlon Brando and Red Buttons, and they needed some Americans to play bit roles. The football season was over and, since I was one of the very few normal-size men on the team, I was cast as a military policeman. At this point in my life, I had never considered becoming an actor.

But, as I watched Brando work, I became intrigued with his method of acting. The characters he created came alive on the set. I was tremendously impressed by his ability to be so original in reciting a prepared text, and I wanted to know how he did it. During the filming, a snowstorm hit the city of Kyoto and stopped production, giving me the opportunity to spend time alone with Brando. We had long discussions about the craft of acting, and I even began to think I might like to try it. I was too much in awe of him to ask, "How do you do it," so I decided to try to do it myself.

The night before he was to shoot the dramatic highlight of the movie, a scene in which he discovers the bodies of Red Buttons and Miyoshi Umeki, who committed suicide rather than let the Army separate them, I took the script to my barracks and studied it. As written, Brando's only line upon discovering the bodies was, "Oh. Oh." Just that simple expression of disbelief, o-h, o-h. I tried to figure out every possible way he could make those sounds, starting high, starting low, going up and down, staying on one tone, and what I thought to be every conceivable variation. I sat around all night repeating, "Oh, oh."

Just before shooting was ready to begin the next day, Brando walked off by himself for a few moments and appeared to be in deep thought. I assumed he was reviewing his lines for the whole scene. When filming started, I watched carefully. When the time came for him to utter his line, he did it in a way different from any I had considered. The two sounds came out mournfully, painfully, a low guttural moan coming from deep inside. Every person on the set could feel the real pain Brando's character experienced.

I had to find out how he had decided on that particular reading. He explained that it wasn't a reading, that he never did readings. Instead he tried to find the emotion that motivated each line. What was the character feeling that made him say whatever he did. In this case, the condition of the character was intense pain, sadness, and an overwhelming feeling of futility. Knowing this, Brando searched his own life for an experience that had caused the same mixture of emotions, and the feeling in that scene came from a sense memory he created. Although he was speaking lines from a script, the emotion he was feeling was very real.

Whether intuitively or through his work at the Actor's Studio, Brando managed to retain access to his own emotions. His ability to project intensity and potential volatility to the audience has always been part of his charisma. Since that time in Japan, I've learned that anyone can regain use of their emotions. By doing so, and learning how to project your real feelings to the world, you can become a more interesting, dynamic person, as well as gain control over your own life. By gaining access to your emotions you begin to act on what *you* really need and want, instead of the desires of the supporting characters of your life.

The memory of everything that has ever happened to us exists in the levels previously mentioned, the intellectual, emotional, and physical. The mind remembers the facts, the body remembers the feelings. If once you almost drowned, for example, you can intellectually explain it in every detail: what you did to save your life, how you struggled, what thoughts raced through your mind as you struggled, and the physical feelings you remember experiencing. But while you're telling this story your stomach may knot up, your legs may suddenly feel weak, your arms may become weary, as your body, your emotional memory, recalls the absolute terror you felt. This tightness, weakness, and weariness is your body's way of describing the same incident the mind describes in words. This emotion is the language of the body. Anyone who has been hit, or nearly hit, by an automobile and tenses up or breaks out in sweat at the sound of brakes squealing forever after is experiencing the same kind of emotional memory.

If you can learn to use your emotions to "tell" the story to the emotions of the people around you, it will be much more effective. Your experience will be communicated on more than a verbal level. You will be bringing more of yourself to that moment. This ability to communicate a full experience through your emotions is an important aspect of what we are attempting to recover.

It is absolutely possible. Actors work at it every day. They practice communicating sense memories the same way a baseball player takes batting practice. That same emotional memory that exists for crisis situations records everything we experience, and does not necessarily need the intellectual memory to trigger it. The body can "remember" those events that so terrified the emotions, that caused so much emotional pain that the mind completely took over. That memory is hidden somewhere. To find those places and release the tension, a form of irrigation is necessary. When a river flows it collects debris, rotted stumps, tin cans, bottles, and garbage. When feeling begins flowing through the body, it collects all the emotional debris, all the rotted stumps and garbage of past experience and opens channels to get rid of it all through the voice and body.

The body is the actor's instrument. It is the vehicle for his performing. It is the housing for his emotions. The more an actor knows his own body, the better able he will be to create a complete characterization. The next exercise is one actors use to bring attention to their body. It is an overall scanning exercise.

It is necessary to study your body, to bring attention to the parts, so you can once again become aware of the range of possibilities that exist within yourself. In a later chapter we will examine the use of the body in actions, but here we are just becoming reacquainted with it. Many people take their bodies, like their ability to change, for granted. They know it is there, but unless there is a crisis situation, a pain or illness, they pay little attention to it. Can you close your eyes and imagine your back? You know something is there, but can you conceive of what it looks like? Or your foot? You probably haven't "experienced" your foot since you were a baby. You see it. It goes with you wherever you go. You would miss it if you woke up one morning and it wasn't there, but you treat it like a foreign object. You have no tactile or sensory relationship with that foot. This exercise is a means of bringing attention to all parts of your body.

RELAXATION EXERCISE

Sit in a comfortable position. An upright position is preferable. It is neither necessary nor desirable to take a lotus position or anything irregular or uncomfortable. After reading all the instructions for this exercise, close your eyes. This is simply to allow you to focus full attention on different areas of your body. In the same way you brought your attention to your breath, scan your entire body. What does it feel like? What does it look like?

Now, direct all your attention to the big toe on your left foot. Think about it's appearance. Feel it. Move it up and down and feel the sensation running through it. Do the same with each toe on your left foot.

Now, bring awareness to the ball of your left foot. Again, try to imagine what it looks like. Feel the sensations in it. Feel its shape.

Do the same for the arch of your left foot. And the heel. And ankle. Spend a moment "with" each different part of your foot. Then try to feel the whole composition of the foot. Feel all the parts moving together. Put weight on your left foot. How does it feel? This is something you do thousands of times each day, but you are rarely aware of the fact that all types of feelings happen in the foot.

Do the same thing for your left calf and knee. Concentrate your full attention on your left thigh. Move your left foot up and down and feel the relationship between the various parts of your left leg.

Starting with the big toe on your right foot, do exactly the same thing for your right leg. When you have completed that, bring this awareness to both legs and their parts at the same time. You may even feel a slight tingling sensation in your legs.

"Feel" the fingers of your left hand. Move them slightly and feel the sensation. Concentrate on the palm of your hand. Does it itch? Now be aware of the composition of your left hand as a whole. Do the same for your wrist, forearm, elbow, and upper arm. Finally, bring your attention to your whole arm.

Do exactly the same exercise for your right arm.

As you relax the different parts of your body during this exercise, you may begin to get drowsy. You might even fall asleep. It does happen, and it is perfectly acceptable. This is a relaxation, sensory exercise.

Bring your full, concentrated attention to your hips, and then the front and back of your body. Then bring that attention to your groin area, and your stomach. Feel the sensation in the center of your body around your navel. Now move that awareness up to your chest area. What does it "feel" like?

"Feel" your shoulders. Tension often exhibits itself in rigid shoulders and jaw muscles. Is there tension in your shoulders? Let them relax. Let them sag. You may feel the tension running right out of your shoulders.

Bring this attention to your lower back and then your upper back.

Try to feel the whole composition of the parts of your

body, your legs, feet, hands, arms, and torso as they radiate sensation.

Now, concentrate your full attention on your neck. Can you "feel" your Adam's apple? Do the same for your jaw. Shake your jaw slightly to feel the sensation of movement. How many times each day do you open and close your mouth without being aware of any feeling in your jaw?

Bring your attention to the area of your mouth. Let your lips relax entirely; allow the tension out of your lips by bringing awareness to them. Now be aware of your nose. Inhale and exhale through your nose and be "with" that feeling. Concentrate your awareness on your eyes, and then finally on your forehead.

Try to bring all these feelings of your body together. Sit quietly and "feel" your body. Let it relax.

WORD SOURCE EXERCISE

Now, with your full attention focused on the feelings in your body, say the word "child" out loud. Don't do anything else. See what happens. If you feel a swelling of emotion, allow it to happen. Don't stop the emotion.

Say the word "fear." Just say it once. See if your body responds in any way. If there is an emotional response, allow it to happen. At this point your feelings are very tentative and can be easily blocked by your mind. You must allow your feelings to be completed. If tears form in your eyes, do not wipe them away, let them fall. Allow your sensitized body to react to the imagery and emotion these words might arouse.

Quietly, say the word "alone."

Say the word "hurt."

Say the word "feeling."

Your mind prevents you from expressing your emotions. To circumvent this, you must ignore the commands of your mind to stop the feeling. You must allow your body to experience whatever reaction you have to these simple words. At first you may have little or no reaction at all—your emotions are frozen and must be thawed—but you should feel the stirring of emotion. This is the beginning of feeling. Later we will use other exercises to magnify that feeling.

This is one of the most common classroom exercises. All my work begins with thawing the frozen feelings of my students. The following excerpt comes from an early exercise I did with an overweight, rather plain-looking woman in her mid-thirties.

WARREN: What are you feeling now?

STUDENT: *(Pause)* I'm feeling silly. This is silly. And nervous.

WARREN: Are you aware of the vibration in your legs?

STUDENT: *(Looking down—both legs are shaking nervously—she laughs)* No.

WARREN: I want to tell you something. It is okay to feel whatever you are feeling right this minute. That is very important. At this moment you don't have to feel any one thing. There are no right or wrong feelings. They are just feelings. You are not in a structured situation in which you're supposed to be pleasant or happy. Right now you are free to feel whatever is going on in your body. Would you say the word "fear" please.

STUDENT: *(Breathing deeply)* Fear. *(No facial reaction, but her legs continue to vibrate)*

WARREN: Lower your chin, please. Continue to breathe steadily. There is plenty of feeling inside you. It's there, we just have to find it. We have to move something out of the way right now. Please keep breathing steadily. Hear what is happening in your body. Would you say the word "sensitive," please.

STUDENT: Sensitive. *(She bites her lower lip as she says it, and a tear forms in her eye. She wipes it away with her hand)*

WARREN: Don't do that please. Leave the feeling alone. Don't stop the feeling. At some point in your life, when you were at ease, vulnerable, spontaneous, someone criticized you or struck you or frightened you or left you. This person violated your feelings. Lift your chin, please. Your emotion is trapped inside, still waiting for permission from that person to come out. Still waiting to feel safe and secure. The idea is to free the emotion so it doesn't have to wait for that person, then everybody will no longer be a reflection of that person. Would you say the word "Mommy."

STUDENT: Mommy. *(Both legs are now vibrating)*

WARREN: Again, please.

STUDENT: Mommy. *(Tears roll from one eye down her face)*

WARREN: Holding all your feelings back is like carrying a great emotional weight. Imagine when you were a little girl someone handed you a big rock and asked you to hold it until they came back. You just kept waiting and waiting and holding the rock. You clothe it, dress it up, paint it, so that it is hard to see that you are holding a rock. Now you have to drop it. Let it go. You can't hold on to it anymore. The person who gave it to you is never going to come back. So you're either going to spend the rest of your life holding the rock they gave you, or you're going to become your own person.

(The student is crying now)

Would you say the word "pain," please.

STUDENT: Pain. *(She repeats it, with real feeling behind it)* Pain.

Ideally, you should sensitize your body by bringing attention to the various parts a number of times each day, beginning in the morning. It is a method of tuning up your body. By checking the different areas, it is possible to locate those places where tension is building up, and by focusing your attention there, release it.

To feel, you must feel. The mind thinks, it does not feel. You can talk about emotions, or read this chapter about them, or even give a dissertation on them, but for all the good that will do you, you might as well eat this book. If you expect to make any meaningful change in your life, you must allow yourself to experience real emotions once again.

Like this student, you have plenty of feeling inside you. An emotion is registered on your senses, rather than in your mind. The smell of burning leaves is enough to create the sensation of fall. The sound of rain on a window, or the touch of a certain fabric, can create an emotional memory. The strongest memory one of my students had about her father was the aroma of his pipe tobacco. While he was in Europe during World War II, her mother would burn some of the tobacco each night and the aroma created a sense of warmth and security in the house. In fact, we can remember through our senses better than we can through our minds. To find real feeling, we shouldn't look for the feeling, we should look for the sensation that registered that feeling. By remembering the sensory aspects of a moment, it is possible to recreate the emotions you experienced at that time. Every experience you've ever had has been registered in your senses, and those moments can be reconstructed.

This discovery was one of the major contributions made to the theatre by Konstantin Stanislavsky. The great Russian actor-director-producer-theorist realized that theatre could be more effective if the actor was able to inject real emotion into the character he was portraying. He searched his own background to devise a technique to enable any performer to summon emotion.

As a young man, he remembered, he visited the country home of his aunt and uncle. They did not get along well. They were always quarreling, and quite nasty to each other—except during lunch. At lunch they would be polite and endearing. The whole composition of their relationship changed over the lunch table. Stanislavsky wondered why, and found his answer in a fruit bowl.

His aunt and uncle had fallen in love in a peach orchard. As often as possible his aunt placed a bowl of peaches on the lunch table. The scent of the fruit sensorily reminded the couple of their youth, their affair, and their love. The scent incited emotions which made fighting impossible.

Emotions can be recreated by stimulating the senses that originally registered them. It was this type of sensual stimulation that Brando used in his memorable *Sayonara* scene. And it is this type of sensual stimulation that can help you to regain lost feelings. Once you allow your body to be free to feel again, to know that emotions do not result in pain, it will be much easier to experience new emotions. The exercise that follows is a way of summoning up emotion from the past. It is the same exercise actors use to learn the method of making a sense memory.

SENSORY EXERCISE

Most of us go crashing through each day, paying as little attention to the world around us as we do to our bodies. We are confronted with countless sensory impulses without being aware that they are registering on our senses and creating sense memories. Few people really smell the aroma or feel the texture of a cup of coffee. It's just a cup of coffee. But it may well be that soothing, familiar aroma that relaxes you enough to start the day.

Pour a glass of water. It makes no difference whether it is hot or cold. Look at it. Bring the same attention to this glass of water that you earlier brought to your breath and to the various parts of your body. Examine the glass of water closely. Feel the glass. Now feel the water itself. What is its temperature? Tap a finger against the side of the glass. What sound does it make? Is the glass sweating? Does it make your palms wet? Now lift the glass and sip the water. Be aware of all the sensations as you swallow. Try to examine every sensory aspect of that simple glass of water. Bring your full attention to it.

Now, put the glass of water out of sight. Using your imagination, create a glass of water and pick it up again. Try to remember each of the sensory aspects of that glass of water. Try to "see" the water in the glass. Did light glint off the glass? Try to feel the texture of the glass. Try to feel its weight on your hand and wrist. Try to feel the temperature of the water on your fingers again. Is it hot or cold? Is the glass sweating? Lift this imaginary glass of water to your lips and sip it. What does it "taste" like? Explore the glass of water thoroughly in your imagination. Now put it down.

Once again, pick up the real glass of water. Examine it carefully. You should be aware of details you never noticed before. Previously it was just a glass of water. Now it is an object that has certain sensory properties and creates specific sensory memories in different parts of your body. Your hand "remembers" the weight of the glass. Your lips "remember" the sensation of its touch. Your throat "remembers" water flowing over it. By bringing all of its sensory aspects together, you can recompose the glass of water.

Everything around you makes a sensory impression. Objects you rarely notice have color, weight, size, and shape, as well as numerous details like scratches, ripples in the wood, chips, stains, and dust. By bringing your attention to these sensory aspects, you will become more aware of the world around you, and more alive to each moment.

EMOTIONAL MEMORY

From the glass of water we will move to an object in which you invested emotional feeling. This might well be a pet, but it can also be a doll, a room, or something as simple as a blanket. The only thing important is that it be something you had strong emotions about. Use your memory to decide what it might be. The purpose of this exercise is to recall the feelings you had for this object, using the same technique you used to recreate the glass of water, recalling the sensory aspects.

This exercise was particularly effective in finding the emotions of a young actor who seemed void of all feelings. His emotions had been beaten deep inside by his father, and I could not find a spark of real feeling in him. Since I knew he was raised on a farm, I explored that area of his past and asked him if there had been a pet—a dog, a cat, a horse, or something else—that he had been close to. He didn't answer verbally; instead his eyes twitched with a glint of emotion. I worked with him, trying to help him recreate those feelings he had for his pet. Finally, one afternoon, his feelings just broke through the hardened barriers. He suddenly burst into tears and said, in these exact words, "That dog was the only person that ever understood me."

"The only *person* . . ." To him that dog was a human being, someone to talk to, someone who would accept his love and return it. By using his sense memory to remember his feelings for that dog, he opened himself up to experience new feelings. Once he remembered, he could feel; he allowed himself emotions.

Sit in a comfortable chair in a relaxing position. Use your intellectual memory to recall an animal or object or even a place about which you had strong feelings. Concentrate and try to remember every sensory aspect of that pet, object, or place. Remember the size. Close your eyes and visualize its color and shape. If it was a pet remember how it looked at you, or what it felt like when he licked or nuzzled you. Remember the moisture on his nose, the sound he made. Remember what he felt like when you picked him up or touched him. Did his ears perk up when he heard your voice? How did you play with him? What tricks could he perform? Remember his smell. Try to recall his favorite resting place. What did he do when he wanted your attention? Did you have a special whistle, or call? Let your hands remember his weight, allow them to recall his warmth.

Calmly, relaxed, while you are enjoying the sense memory, say his name out loud.

If you invested strong emotion in an inanimate object, try to recall how heavy it was when you picked it up, the particular odor it had, what color it was. Was it old and faded or bright and new? When you carried it, did you feel older? Or did it embarrass you? Remember the feel of the material it was made from. Remember where you put it to keep it safe at night.

Try to remember how proud of it you were, and how you felt the day you received it. Allow your hands to "feel" it once again.

Some of my students have strong emotional investments in a place. Their own room, their parents' bedroom, a park they played in as a child. One of the strongest emotional memories many people carry is that of a hospital in which someone they loved spent time or died. Try to remember a place that frightened you, or made you feel good. What did the place smell like? Was it a strong, pungent odor or a deep, distressing smell? What color were the walls? Can you remember a specific piece of furniture? What was the floor covered with? When you crawled on the floor, was it cold? Was there anything you crawled under and explored? Are there any sounds you remember?

For almost everyone, the dark has a strong emotional attachment. Many parents lock their children in dark rooms. Others actually lock their own children in dark closets. What did the dark mean to you? Try to remember how you felt when your parents turned out the lights at night. Were you frightened? Did you believe monsters lurked outside your windows? Or did you share your room with someone and spend hours talking and dreaming in the dark? Close your eyes and recreate the feelings you had in the dark of the night. Try to "see" your room. Were there venetian blinds on the window that rattled in the night breeze? Could you hear adults talking or laughing in another room? Did you draw your covers up over your head for protection? Everyone has feelings about the darkness. Try to recall them.

You may be experiencing the beginning of emotion. Often it will start as a sensation in your hands or feet as your body remembers a certain unique feeling. These exercises should be enjoyable. Their purpose is to help you remember a real emotion and to allow you to recreate that feeling. They should also be used when you create a personalization.

FULL SENSORY EXERCISE

Now, still comfortably seated, relaxed, bring together all the exercises of this chapter. Begin by bringing attention to the different parts of your body. Then recall a moment when you felt deep emotion. It might have been love, anger, or great sorrow. It is not important to remember the narrative, the "and then, and then." Rather, try to remember the sensory aspects of that moment. It was composed of colors, sounds, tactile feelings, and smells. Let these come into your mind. Allow them to appear, don't make an effort. Feelings must be allowed. The mind does not know how to feel, it thinks; the body knows how to feel. Let it. Remember the people who were present at that moment, the expressions on their faces, the sounds of their voices. Enjoy the memory in your mind, but feel the emotions your body remembers. This is real feeling. This is emotion.

If you've just come home from the office where you had a fight with your boss and had to hold your feelings in, or if you've just separated from someone you love, or if you've recently fallen in love, this exercise should be easy. You should be tingling with feelings. But the emotions this exercise is designed to bring forth you experienced long ago. It is vital to recall these original experiences, the places where your ability to feel freely was first blocked.

You might not be successful in recreating a feeling the first time you try. There are many layers of insulation between your vulnerable feelings and the world. They have been hidden so long it is not easy to locate them. And even after experiencing them, it will still take time to bring them to the surface where they can be translated into action.

If you practice this exercise, you will begin to feel. Some of the emotions you will release may be very painful. There have been many dramatic moments in class as students relived absolutely horrifying moments long buried in their subconscious. But once they brought these emotional memories to the surface, they were finally free of them and their debilitating effects.

How will the ability to recall emotional turmoil enrich your life? It will prove very liberating. By allowing your most painful emotional memories to surface, you will finally be free of the fear they caused, free to experience new emotions. The inability to express what is really going on inside can be debilitating. It makes it impossible for you to take actions based on your own desires. It can cause tension and anxiety and the resulting headaches and body pains. It can cause a general malaise which is manifested in numerous ways, ranging from excess weight to bad posture. And trapped feelings can cause depression.

Simply by allowing your old emotions to surface, you can take control of your life. You will be free to enjoy each moment on both intellectual and emotional levels, and will be able to communicate with other people on these levels.

The exercises explained in this chapter work. With practice, you will be able to reach long-trapped feelings. Eventually you'll begin to reacquire real feeling. Taking actions based on this real feeling will make you feel complete and satisfied, and in control of your own life.

CHAPTER FOUR:
Mind, Emotion, Body—The Parts of Your Part

And thus the native hue of resolution
Is sicklied o'er with the pale cast of thought,
And enterprises of great pitch and moment
With this regard their currents turn awry
And lose the name of action.

—SHAKESPEARE

A farmer had seventeen sheep. All but nine died. How many did he have left? This is an exercise for your mind. It requires no action. It requires no emotion.

Raise one hand into the air. Now lower it. This is an action. It is an exercise for your body. It requires no thought. It requires no emotion.

Make a sense memory, as you learned in Chapter Three, of a crisp fall day. Feel the bite of cool air on your face. Smell the sharp aroma of burning leaves. Imagine the long shadows cast by bare trees. This sense memory should stir some pleasant emotions. It requires no action.

79

Thoughts, actions, and emotions can exist independently. You can think. You can act. You can feel. But nothing will be as effective as using all of these components together. In doing so, you will be bringing a greater part of yourself to any time, any place, any event.

If you are reading and understanding this book, you know how to use your mind. In Chapter Two we discussed actions, how to take them freely, and how to choose the proper ones. Emotions were the subject of Chapter Three, and how to reintroduce them back into the body through exercise.

In this act, we will use exercises to put the feeling into action, to bring the feeling into the world. It is this work that makes my acting workshop unique, and it is this work that will be the key to your regaining the freedom to take actions to satisfy your needs and desires.

Many of my students have learned how to reach their feelings. Some have even been through primal or other therapies. They seem to believe that having had this rich experience somehow equips them to be great artists. That is no more true than a collection of wood and nails is a house. Emotions are the material for action, but having access to your emotions is only one prerequisite for growth.

An intellect is not enough, either. An actor who works from his mind may give a professional performance, but rarely brings anything meaningful, any thrust, any life, to his characterization.

Working from the emotions or the mind is not enough in everyday life, either. Actions without emotional support are often dull or listless. They lack excitement. And emotions are not meant to be held inside. Having contact with your feelings but not expressing them would be like an actor performing in a closet.

The actors who give the most memorable performances, and the people who make the greatest impression on other people, are those who can inject their feelings into actions, they put emotion into motion.

As I've stated before, there is a brief period in your life when your emotions and actions are in harmony. You take actions to carry out your emotional needs. But, as you grow, your mind breaks this connection; it supervises your actions and protects your emotions. And it replaces your natural emotional response with learned behavior. You learn how to act. Through trial and error you learn the proper response to most situations. You learn how to amuse or to tease or to evoke sympathy. You learn how to make love and how to deal with most problems. Your behavior, in fact, becomes habitual. You develop a form of behavior that enables you to react to almost any situation. Eventually you come to believe that all of this knowledge, this habitual way of acting, is what you really are. It is not. This is the person you created as a means of survival. It is the face you put on to meet the world. It is your protection. But it is that creation the world identifies as "you."

People are rarely the image they present. Instead, like an actor puts on a costume, makeup, and steps into a role, they carefully prepare the most positive image possible and try to make the world believe it is really them. No one wants other people to know that, deep inside, they are insecure, or frightened, confused, lonely or unhappy, so they learn how to act happy, confident, and secure. They put on a happy face. They use their intelligence to create an external person as armor to protect the fragile person inside.

This armor has nothing to do with what we really are, really feel, or really want. It is the part we've written for ourselves. It is a carefully prepared illusion which confronts other people's illusions. Most of us go through life lugging this protective armor and constantly wondering why no one really understands us, or why we have such difficulty communicating.

The protective armor was constructed by the mind during childhood. Fitting began the first time our emotions were separated from the corresponding actions, when what we wanted to do was different from what we were permitted to do. To explain this to my students I use the visit of the Dowager Aunt.

The Dowager Aunt is one tough lady. She is overweight, overbearing, and worth over a million dollars. Among the many things she does that you find annoying, she likes to grab your cheek between her thumb and forefinger, twist firmly, pucker up her lips, and proclaim much too loudly in crowded places, "So cute! So cute! I could eat you right up!"

Since that is not a particularly appealing thought, and since your cheek aches for days after every visit, you would like her to stop. The emotion you feel, your condition, is anger. To convey that feeling into action, your intention is to kick her in the leg the next time she begins to pucker and twist.

However, the intention of your parents prevents you from doing this. They want part of that legacy. Their intention is to charm her out of as much of it as they possibly can.

Your desires are in competition with theirs. If you let her have it in the leg, it will become more difficult for your parents to charm her. Since they are bigger and stronger, they are authority figures and have the power to impose their desires upon you. You can't put your emotion into action without penalty.

The next time your Dowager Aunt visits, anger swells inside your body. You can almost see a target printed on her leg. You feel ready to explode. She leans down and grabs a chunk of cheek between her thumb and forefinger and, spitting as she speaks, shrieks, "So cute! So cute! I could eat you up!"

Although your emotions are raging, your mind is issuing warning signals. If you take the wrong action, you will be punished. So you smile and offer her a cup of tea. Later, after your Aunt departs, your parents reward your good behavior with a quarter. They have successfully imposed their behavior patterns on you.

This is where the trouble begins. Childhood is filled with daily conflicts similar to this one. The direct expression of emotion is repressed through fear of punishment or embarrassment, and what you end up doing may have nothing to do with your real feelings. As children, we are all intimidated into fulfilling other people's needs and desires. So by the time we are old enough to take actions without needing consent, we've lost the ability. The natural progression between desire and fulfillment has been shattered. The mind has taken charge.

As a result, as adults, we often have conflicting conditions and intentions, We feel anger but present a charming exterior, or we feel frightened but appear calm. To protect our emotions, we deny they exist. We stop showing emotion. As Woody Allen put it in a movie, "Excuse me while I go into the bathroom and scream."

I see this armor exhibited in class all the time. As soon as I begin talking to a student about his emotional state, his mind tries to change the subject. If I persist and mention key emotional words like "hurt" or "feeling" or "pain," as we did in the exercise in Chapter Three, he becomes very intimidated, frightened. This goes directly back to childhood pain and fear.

I've had students practically crawl up to the stage on their hands and knees, their shoulders drooping, back bent, eyes half-closed, their faces scrunched up and wrinkled. They look as if they were carrying an anchor on their back. But when I ask how they feel, they open their eyes slightly, smile weakly, and say, "I'm fine. Never felt better in my life. I'm a little tired though. Too many wild parties."

A retired star of the New York Jets football team has been studying with me. As an active player he was known for his toughness. The very first time I worked with him I asked him to try to stand very still on the stage and face the members of the class. Although he'd performed on national television in front of millions of people, he found it terribly difficult to just stand still.

I asked him to say the word "tough."

He repeated it firmly.

I asked him to say the word "shy."

He shifted his weight from one foot to the other. He shook his hands, lowered his chin, and said, without feeling, "Shy." I asked him to say it again, more slowly, and to try to feel it as he said it. He raised his chin and did exactly as I asked. And fainted.

Inside, this football star was a tender little boy craving affection. The football uniform was his armor. It allowed him to be tough and unemotional. It provided protection for his real feelings. In fact, he originally began playing football to prove to his father and his peers that he wasn't shy or sensitive, when that was precisely what he was.

Playing football permitted him to release the energy his emotions produced that would otherwise have been expressed as some form of tension. Since most of us lack his ability to play professional football, we have to find other means to release that energy. Normally we do this by substituting socially acceptable behavior for the actions we'd really like to carry out. It is considered poor manners, for example, to express anger by slamming someone over the head with a stick, so the energy your anger produces is either stored in the body as tension or expressed through a totally unconnected action. This acceptable action can be anything from a nervous tic to the steady tapping of your foot. In this way many aspects of individual character are formed, habits you learn to identify as "me." Thus the quiet bookkeeper, loved by everyone, who never says a nasty word, who is always smiling, spends the entire day playing with her hair, plucking eyebrows, cracking her knuckles, tapping both feet, banging her knees together, and pulling at one earlobe. These habits have nothing to do with what she is really like, they are just part of her armor. Each action has a meaning in her private vocabulary.

It's fun to watch celebrities perform and to interpret their body language. Sammy Davis, Jr.'s anger takes the form of humor and self-abuse. When someone says something that is in some way offensive to him, he'll put his head down, start lifting his legs, and actually hit himself. He doesn't let you see his face, which might give away traces of his real feelings. Johnny Carson expresses his anger or embarrassment by fixing his tie or his jacket. Watch him. He sits behind a desk, appearing to be totally at ease, while his great comic mind is working furiously. But when he is unnerved, his hand goes to his tie. What he is really doing is fixing his feelings. You, and all the members of your supporting cast, have also developed personal ways of fixing your feelings. Often you identify this behavior as a habit. In reality, it is part of your armor. It is part of the way you protect your emotions.

These small actions are vitally important for survival. Without using them to help release some of the tension that builds up during the day, we would be walking emotional time bombs. And, eventually, something might happen to trigger an explosion.

The proper way to release tension is to carry out an action that conveys your real emotion. When you are angry, you should express it. When you are in love, you should express it. It is the means you choose to express it that is important. Every emotion can be conveyed through a number of different actions. The most volatile of all emotions, anger, can be shown by hitting someone, or just hitting out with your hands, or screaming, challenging, threatening, and cursing. Your anger will be released in each instance. Your external anger will convey your feeling and the energy will be expelled.

To regain this innate ability to translate emotion into action, the original connections have to be reestablished. Because pain caused these links to be broken, it is sometimes painful to put them back together. The most difficult part of my work is convincing students that the results are worth risking pain for. The more you allow yourself to remember the original causes of your emotional pain, using the exercises in this book to help you, the stronger the new link between your emotions and your actions will be.

These exercises will help you to rid yourself of pain that exists inside. Don't be frightened by the pain you may experience. It is pain flowing out, not being inflicted. It's as if you were pulling arrows shot into you so long ago you've become convinced they were always there. You've even started using them as coat racks. It's going to hurt when you pull them out; it's going to take some getting used to. This is a healing process.

For actors, this pain can be particularly valuable material to draw on. When a young actress, Jessica Lang, began working in class, it was obvious she was holding back a great deal of emotion. Through exercise work she learned how to release much of it. I remember telling her that if she ever had a successful career she should be thankful to whoever caused all her fear and suffering. So the first role she won was as a screaming, fearful leading lady opposite King Kong.

Donna McKechnie, the award-winning star of *A Chorus Line*, used some of the disappointments in her life for the role she created in that show. She is an enormously talented actress, but professionally had been categorized as a dancer. She just couldn't get work as an actor. In classroom exercises she worked to feel the despair and anguish in her body—to put the links back together. Eventually she was able to articulate these feelings through her body. When she talks about herself in *Chorus Line*, she is using material she discovered in the classroom.

By allowing emotions back into your body, actions you could not previously carry out suddenly become possible. The same person who could only tease or entice becomes capable of commanding, demanding, threatening, expressing real anger or real love. To do this it is necessary to learn how to take the emotion you feel and convey it, using your voice and body, into an action.

Remember, before you understood the meaning of words, you took actions. These actions were your only language, your only means of communicating. You could push away or hold, strike out or snuggle, or take any number of basic actions to satisfy your needs and desires. In order to rediscover and utilize this language of emotion-action that existed before conscious thought, it is necessary to get around the mind.

Only your basic needs could be expressed in this language. The first action a child learns is to wave good-bye. At one point in life this action is a complete vocabulary. All the feelings and knowledge of the child are expressed through this action.

I remember the first time I included this action in an exercise. I asked a student to make a personalization of the individual on whom he had been most dependent. Once he had accomplished that, I told him to wave good-bye to that person. "I don't want you to say anything," I explained. "Just wave your hand good-bye." Almost immediately his hands began trembling and tears welled up in his eyes. His body remembered the terrible feeling of abandonment he had felt as a child. His body remembered this feeling his mind had repressed. Since that day I've worked to develop a set of exercises to recover the whole vocabulary of this first language.

The basic needs we are able to express in this language include:

I want
I need
I take
I give
come back
get away

**mine
yours
let me go
don't leave me
hold me
'bye**

The actions are basic. To order "I want" or "I need" the child holds out the palms of his hand and draws them into his chest.

"Get away" is expressed by raising your hands against your shoulders, palms facing forward, elbows back, then thrusting out from both elbows as hard as possible.

"I take" or "mine" is conveyed as an action by reaching straight out with an open hand, clamping it tightly closed, then drawing it back quickly and firmly against your chest.

" 'Bye" is spoken by holding both arms straight out and just waving your arms and fingers. Your arms should be kept straight and you should wave from your wrists.

The action meaning "come back" or "don't leave me" is just the opposite. Hold your hands out, palms facing upward, and try to signal the person to come back by waving your hands and fingers inward, toward your body.

"Hold me" is a simple matter of raising your arms as if you wanted to be picked up by an adult.

"Yours" and "I give," words developed later in this vocabulary, are expressed by holding your fists against your chest, then stretching out your arms as you open your hands.

These simple exercises will allow you to convey emotions precisely as you expressed them before you knew how to verbalize them. Using them while making personalizations will enable some people to feel emotions being released almost immediately; other people will take more time. Women, my experience has shown, have easier access to their emotions than men. This is as would be expected in a society that equates a demonstration of emotion in men with weakness. But eventually these exercises will work for everybody. I've never had a student come into my workshop, and stay there, who did not respond to these exercises. You work; they work.

Now we will combine all the material included in the first four acts. Now is the time for you to play with them. Your goal is to produce real emotion and then express it through an action.

MIND-EMOTION-BODY EXERCISE

During this exercise it will be easier to remain standing. Using the sensitivity technique, relax your body. As you learned earlier, start with your toes and bring your attention to each part of your body. Feel the tension flowing out of your shoulders as you relax them. Relax your jaw. Bring your awareness to your legs, upper body, arms, neck, then head. Your body should be relaxed.

Now begin making a personalization—remember the person you were most dependent upon as a child. Use the same sensory techniques you used to recreate a glass of water. Remember, you are trying to recall the impression this person made on your emotions, not your mind. You are creating a sensory image, not an intellectual memory, so allow your senses to remember this person. Remember how this person looked; the color of their hair, the quality of their complexion. Try to recall the sound of their voice. Inhale deeply and remember the scents that surrounded them. Remember how good you felt when they smiled at you, how comfortable and loved.

Remember how difficult it was for you to stand up to this person. Try not to think about these things. Don't let thoughts come between your emotions and your body. Just feel these things.

Now, say the name you called them out loud. Call them.

Ask them nicely to come to you. Speak to them. If you cannot find the right words, if you're just not capable of speaking to them, speak to them in numbers, but speak from the emotion you are feeling.

Now, remember how this person hurt you. How much you wanted them to hold you, but how hard it was for you to tell them that.

EMOTIONAL APPEAL

Hold your hands straight out in front of you, palms facing upward. Use both your hands and your voice to call them to you. Wave them closer with your fingers. Your emotions will remember. You don't have to do anything at all. If your hands or jaw start to vibrate slightly, please do nothing to stop that. Allow it to happen. Don't let your mind interfere.

Wave your fingers inward and ask this person to come to you. Let your hands remember who they wanted to reach out to. If there are sounds welling from inside your body, please don't stop them. Allow them to happen.

EMOTIONAL DEMAND

Relax your arms. Bring your hands up against your shoulders, palms facing away from your body, then thrust them out, hard. Snap your elbows. As you do this, change your tone. Demand that this person "get away!" Say it out loud. Snap your hands out and demand it. Repeat this action and demand a number of times. Now talk to this person from this feeling. Tell them those things you were never able to before. Tell them how they hurt you. Don't be afraid to get angry at them. Don't worry if you mumble or your sentences don't make sense. Snap your arms out. Tell them, "Get away from me!" Let them feel your anger. Tell them they had no right to treat you the way they did.

Don't stop any vibration you may experience.

Tell them not to touch you again. They don't own you anymore. Tell them you are free to do whatever you want, they can't stop you. Express your anger.

EMOTIONAL COMMAND

Now, relax. Take a deep breath. Let your arms fall to your side. Then reach out as far as you can with an open hand, close that hand into a fist, then quickly draw it in against your chest. As you do this, state authoritatively, "*I* take." And as you complete this action a second time, "Mine." Repeat this a number of times then, speaking from the emotion, the anger, tell that person what *you* want. Tell them you want to be loved. Tell them you want to be held. Tell them you want to be treated fairly. Don't think about these things. Allow your body to remember the feelings. Your body knows who you are talking to. Keep telling that person what *you* want. What you deserve. Try to find the words in the emotion. At first this may be difficult, but eventually the words will come.

EMOTIONAL PLEA

Once again, relax completely. Let your hand fall to your side. Then straighten both arms out in front of you and, from your wrists, wave good-bye. Let your fingers be free. Wiggle them. Feel the emotion in your hands. Your hands know who they are saying good-bye to. They remember the pain, the feeling of loss, the terror you felt. As you do this, in a calm voice, tell this person how much you need them. Please keep waving. If tears come, don't stop them, don't wipe them away. Let your shoulders relax. Let your jaw relax. Talk to this person from what you are feeling right now. Express that feeling through your voice and body. Find your own words to tell them how much you love them, and don't want them to ever leave you alone.

Keep waving from your wrist. Plead with them not to go away. Speak to them the way you wanted to, but somehow just could not. Don't be afraid. There is nothing to be afraid of anymore. Let your hands remember the feeling. Now tell this person how much you love them. Tell them how much you need them. Wave good-bye to them. Tell them good-bye.

Please relax. Bring your full attention to the feelings flowing through your body. Be aware of how you are feeling right now. Take deep breaths and be "with" your breath. Bring your attention to your breath, to the starting place. This exercise is now completed.

This exercise should have allowed you to experience feelings and express them through your voice and body. Eventually it should not be necessary for you to use this exercise to evoke emotions, rather they will result from the daily conflicts you experience in the world. But this exercise will help reconnect the wires between emotion and action. It will allow you to feel how you should be expressing your emotions to the world. It will also allow you to complete intentions you started long ago and could not complete that have been preventing you from experiencing real feeling since then.

You have found ways of dealing with the world. You have survived. But the person you present to the world is not really you. These feelings you experienced doing this exercise are essentially you. When you wave good-bye, you are utilizing your emotions and your body and your mind. The function of the mind is to help you carry out the action, not to interpret the emotion. When you are capable of bringing real emotion to the world through your body with the aid of your mind, the person to whom it is directed will also experience it on these levels. You will be bringing all of yourself to that moment.

There are times to speak primarily from the intellect and times to speak primarily from the emotion. When you are required to make a decision that involves previous knowledge, facts that you know, the intellect should make the decision. But when telling another person you love them, or hate them, or need them, or desire them, or sympathize with them, your emotions should speak. The words you choose and the actions you take should be dictated by your emotions.

This exercise should be repeated often. The first time you feel emotions begin flowing through your body you will appreciate its value. Properly utilized, this exercise will help you to rediscover frozen feelings and enable you to show them to the world, freeing you to experience new emotions. Eventually, you will be able to do this with a second person. Each of you will be able to make a personalization, then improvise a dialogue expressing the same feelings and actions.

If you have great difficulty finding words to express the emotions you are feeling, turn to the monologues included at the end of the book and put your feelings into one of them.

Incidentally, the answer to the mind-bender that opened this chapter is simple. If all but nine of the farmer's sheep died, he had nine sheep left.

CHAPTER FIVE:
The Ultimate Instrument

Suit the action to the word,
the word to the action.

—SHAKESPEARE

On the first magnificent afternoon of a recent spring, I was in my apartment being interviewed for a magazine article. Although the publicity was important for my workshop, I couldn't focus my mind on the questions. It was invitingly bright and warm outside, and after the long winter my body was aching to be in the sunshine. So I squirmed in my chair, unable to concentrate. My body was demanding immediate attention.

I stood up in the middle of a question. "I know you're going to think I'm crazy," I told the reporter, "but I have to go take a shower right now."

I left the room and took a quick, cool, satisfying shower.

It completely relaxed my body. I was able to return to the interview and bring my full attention to each question.

The body is the third and least demanding part of the triumvirate. Until it breaks down, or until its appearance begins changing, most of us take it for granted. Only when something goes wrong with it does it get primary consideration. But, like our mind and emotions, the healthy body has real needs that must be satisfied. Unless they are, it operates at less than fullest capacity, making it impossible for you to bring your complete attention to any action.

The body is the workhorse of the emotions and the intellect. Its primary functions are to carry out actions commanded by the mind and to provide an outlet for the expression of emotions. It plays the primary role in sexual attraction and relationships. And it serves as your omnipresent identification tag, the physical presentation you make to the world. People identify you by describing your body.

Your changing physical appearance has a tremendous impact on the development of your character and will be discussed thoroughly in Chapter Six. In this chapter we deal with the body and voice as essential tools for communicating your needs, desires, and thoughts.

The human body is the ultimate instrument of expression. It is to an actor what a piano is to a musician, the machinery he uses to express his talent to an audience. But the actor is both the player *and* piano, and the success of his performance depends on both the virtuosity of the player and the condition of the instrument. No matter how talented the player is, if he is performing on a less than adequate instrument, he will be unable to give his finest performance. The quality of the instrument is as important as the ability of the player.

Getting the most out of your life is as much an art as music or acting. Your body is the instrument through which you express this art. The better conditioned your instrument, the more completely you will be able to express what

you want and how you are feeling. No matter how in touch
with your feelings you are, no matter how well developed
your intellectual capabilities, if you don't have control of
your instrument you won't be able to communicate your
feelings and intentions thoroughly.

Part of keeping this physical instrument in tune involves
the mechanics of taking care of the body. This is not an exercise or diet book, but the importance of a regular exercise
program and careful eating behavior cannot be overempha-
sized. Regular medical checkups are also important. An un-
healthy body can easily upset the balance you're working to
create between your three parts.

Many people forget the importance of keeping their body
finely tuned. As ridiculous as it seems, they take their
physical condition for granted. They are always ready to begin a reducing or conditioning program, but never seem to
start. Amazingly, actors are among the worst offenders.
These are people whose careers depend on keeping their instruments in top shape, yet many of them do nothing about
it. At a party I attended in honor of famed violinist Eric
Friedman, most of the guests were actors. After Friedman
performed, I watched him lovingly care for his violin. He
cleaned it carefully, then gently put it in a safe place. It occurred to me that he was taking better care of his wooden
violin than the actors were taking care of their instruments.
They were drinking too much, eating too much, and staying up too late. It reminded me how many promising or
flourishing careers have been destroyed through misuse of
the body and made me wonder how many nonperformers
fail because they have no understanding of the care and use
of their instruments.

A great deal of my work is concentrated on the body. Not
only its physical appearance, which changes as the work
progresses, but on its function as a means of communication. The body talks. It expresses, it reinforces. The exercises I've developed in the classroom help tune the body.

They are to be used the same way a musician uses scales, as a prelude to a performance.

There are many techniques that enable people to regain contact with their feelings, but most work stops there. And feeling alone, without being able to share it, is not enough. The exercises you learned in the previous chapter will enable you to communicate that feeling through your body.

Your body is always speaking. A tremendous amount of all your conversation is visual. If you put plugs in your ears and we had a conversation, you would not be able to hear me, but you would be able to read me with your eyes. Through my posture, the expression on my face, the attitude of my eyes, and the movements of my arms and hands, you would be able to visually understand. You would know if I was happy or unhappy, relaxed, in distress, energetic, tired, upset, concerned, nervous, intent, preoccupied, uncomfortable, or depressed. The better able my body was to express my emotions, the greater my visual vocabulary would be. The entire silent movie industry depended on an actor's ability to express language emotion visually, but when the "talkies" began, this art was abandoned. Because we can communicate verbally, we forget the importance of this additional language. In order to communicate my thoughts and emotions completely, both my body and voice must be "talking." And, while you were listening, I would be able to read your reactions through your body.

There are a large number of universally understood body signals you use without even being aware you are communicating. An open palm generally means friendship or cooperation, a closed fist anger or intensity. The difference between a smile and frown is obvious. A person who keeps his arms folded and legs close together is closing off his body from communication.

When I first came to New York City to study at Actor's Studio, I worked tending bar to survive. Almost every afternoon a middle-aged woman would come into the place, more, I think, to converse with the friendly bartender than for the few drinks she would have. Eventually she began to confide in me, in that unusual way people confide in strangers. Most of the time she talked about the man she was seeing. It was obvious that her feelings for him were stronger than his feelings for her. Everytime she began to talk about her feelings, I noticed she would involuntarily close her eyes. She might say, " . . . and, of course, I don't really care about him at all," and her eyes would clamp shut. "Personally," she would begin, closing both eyes and communicating to me that she was going to talk about him, "I don't care how he feels about me, because I have no feelings for him." Her body language told me that her voice was lying.

Watching this woman, I began to understand that you reveal as many feelings through your body as you do through your voice. Occasionally these signals are obvious, like crunching up your nose in distaste, or a mother clutching at her chest to indicate the heartache her children are giving her, but most are more subtle and rarely read by others. Knowing that a person's true feelings are revealed or concealed by his body can be very beneficial. If you are trying to impress someone and you notice their vision drifting away from you, or they continually shift their body, it should be a signal for you to change your line of conversation. It's not working for you. Or if someone has the ability to intimidate you simply by their size or their tough expression, or even their attractiveness, eliminate visual communication completely. Use the telephone until you feel secure enough to deal with them.

A problem many people have, without even realizing it, is that they communicate information with their body which contradicts what they are saying. They may, for example, be explaining how calm and confident they are, but their hands will be shaking, their skin cold and clammy, and their eyes half-closed. This body language is as accurate as anything they say to you.

These "private gestures," this personal vocabulary, is an important aspect of an actor's technique. As the voice speaks, the body expresses the meaning of the words. And when the body and voice, the emotions and the mind, work together, you actually *become the word*. Every part of you expresses and reinforces the word. Good playwriting is rich in animate, descriptive text that enables the body to "verbalize" at the same time the words are being spoken. The audience not only hears what the actor is saying, it also sees it. The embodiment of this is Katherine Hepburn. Her body is always active, and is always perfectly balanced between verbal and visual expression. Her body simultaneously describes the words as she speaks them, making it very difficult for the audience to take its attention away from her. In her movies, but particularly during her rare television appearances, Katherine Hepburn is a symphony, a rhapsody, or perfectly amalgamated voice and body. Few people are capable of using their bodies so expressively.

One of the most effective performances I have seen was given by an unknown actor in an Off-Broadway production of Eugene O'Neill's classic *Moon for the Misbegotten*. Playing the role of the lovable, drunken Irish father, he would lift his index finger to his nose and rub it every time he was telling an outrageous lie. It became a signal to the audience—when he lifted his finger a big lie was coming. Finally, at the conclusion of the play, his daughter can no longer bear his drinking and lying and castigates him for destroying her life. He starts to answer her with his normal bombast, his hand once more reaching up toward his nose. But halfway there, it stopped, hung momentarily in midair, straining to go forward but held back by some invisible force, and finally dropped slowly back into his lap. The gesture was incredibly effective. The audience had just seen the symbolic death of the human spirit, and the point was

made more effectively than O'Neill's words alone would
have been able to make it.

Unfortunately, developing the ability to communicate
through this second language is as neglected as silent movies. Returning to our original concept, as a child you conveyed your first feelings through actions. These actions
brought your emotions to the attention of the people you
wanted to communicate with. Unfortunately, when these
needs and desires were ignored or rebuffed, you lost much
of the freedom of body movement associated with them.
You learned to put thoughts before actions.

Our highly structured national educational system rein-
forced this tendency. Designed to educate as many children
as efficiently as possible, the system requires strict disci-
pline and, while the ends are constructive, the means are
often destructive. Children are taught to be part of a group,
to be quiet and agreeable. Independent thought is frequently discouraged because it tends to make teaching a whole
class more difficult than it already is. Movement is also severely restricted. Sitting up, sitting straight, and sitting quietly are instructions hammered into children from their
first day of nursery school. In 1977 a child was even sus-
pended from school because he didn't sit up straight *on the
school bus*! Of necessity, the body is robbed of totally free
movement, and the child who expresses himself through
his body is often criticized. Eventually, because it is easier
to survive by going along with the system, most children
restrict themselves to acceptable body movement.

The result is a society of people only partially able to
communicate with the rest of the world. People who are
not even aware that their body is an important, effective
mode of communicating emotions and reinforcing their
voice.

The body is the perfect vehicle for expressing your emotions. When it is not used for that purpose it becomes stat-
ic. It lacks vitality. There is absolutely none of the so-called

magic ingredient every actor craves, charisma. Unless your body is exercised regularly, movement becomes more and more restricted.

The same is true for our other method of social communication, the voice. The voice is the strings of the instrument. It is produced by the lungs, larynx, pharynx, nose, and mouth and is really nothing more than a burst of air being pushed outward through a series of chambers to make sounds. These sounds are similar to tones produced by an orchestra. But when they are cut and sliced into patterns, they become symbols, "words," and are used to express speicific thoughts. The word is only a representation of a thought. The words "fear" and "lost," for example, are only sounds, but have been given far greater meaning.

The texture of the voice is as important in saying a word as the sound itself. It should be rich with changes of level, emphasis, and vibrancy. Emotion is expressed through the sound of the voice, not the words it forms. A voice full of excitement, awe, sorrow, or happiness captures so much more attention than a banal, scratchy, or thin voice. Richard Burton's trained melodious voice is responsible for much of the attention he attracted early in his career. Using your voice to reinforce your chosen words is a vital part of injecting your entire character with vitality.

Yet for many people this is not possible. One of the first things people do to disguise their feelings is to edit their voice. They take all emotion out of it, making it impossible to tell what they are feeling. Instead, they learn to speak in a single, boring register.

The voice is easily inhibited. When children are abused, ignored, ordered to speak or to be silent, they can easily become embarrassed about their own presence. So they do everything possible to not attract any attention. The result of this is often a voice totally lacking in vitality. For an actor this is a disaster. An actor without the ability to express emotions through his voice is like a concert violinist performing on an instrument with only three strings. On the other hand, a vibrant voice like that of Carol Channing or James Cagney or even Bella Abzug can be the key to an entire career.

One of America's most respected actors was already a major star when he began studying with me. He had spent years teaching himself how to enunciate clearly and to speak from the diaphragm, and had developed a mellow, resonant voice. He also went through different types of primal and emotional therapies and gained access to his emotions. But when he started to speak, none of the emotion he was feeling went into his voice. No matter what he was feeling inside, unless he spoke softly or shouted, he sounded basically the same all the time. He could speak and he could feel, but he could not integrate the two.

There was nothing I could teach him about theatre technique. My job was to reconnect his emotions to his voice. To accomplish this, I used exactly the same exercise described in Chapter Four. Summoning up emotions by making a personalization, using his voice to command or to challenge and his hands to express the intention physically, all his parts began working together. He began to convey his emotional condition through his body and the quality of his voice, and his thoughts through word selection.

Almost all my students experience some change in their voice quality while working with me. The initial changes occur when they realize the importance of their voice to their profession and begin paying attention to its quality. Then, as they eliminate some of the tension in their body, they open up their throat and lose the stridency produced by restricted vocal cords. As they learn to speak from their emotions, the voice begins to reclaim the texture that has been edited out.

I used to refer to one of my students as the WAC Sergeant. I didn't do this to be cruel. I did it to bring her attention to her voice. It was gruff and demanding, without any semblance of warmth. I asked her if she remembered any songs from childhood. She stood thinking for a moment; then her face brightened with a smile. "One," she said, "I used to sing it in kindergarten. It was 'I'm a Little Teapot.' "

"Would you sing it for us now?" I asked.

She laughed, slightly embarrassed, and with a little more prodding began singing. Suddenly her voice was high, light, delicate. She was a child again. Her whole facial disposition changed. " . . . pour me out . . . " she finished, and then asked in her old deep, cold voice, "How was that?"

The class laughed out loud at the contrast of the two voices of this one person.

From that moment on, I had her sing all her lines in every scene she did, in the same singsong style used in grammar school. Eventually that fun, lilting voice began creeping into her normal speaking voice until her gruff, unfeeling quality disappeared.

Voice quality is extremely important and you should pay attention to the sound of your own voice. For fun, sing one of your favorite childhood songs. Listen to your voice as you do, and contrast it to your normal speaking voice. Other people will be quick to categorize you, based on the sound of your voice alone, and you must aware of that. A woman who speaks in a breathy tone is likely to be considered in sexual terms. A woman who speaks with a husky voice will be given respect. For a man, a deep voice is considered a sign of masculinity, and a high voice effeminate. By bringing your attention to your voice, you can make some basic changes. By allowing your emotions to be expressed through your voice, you can permanently make your voice more exciting. And by relaxing your body, using the sensory exercises, you can also relax your voice.

Your voice should further your intention. If you want to be commanding, it should be firm. If you want to be sympathetic, it should be soft. But when you mix voice tone and intention the result is often chaos. As much as Paul Lynde might like to appear authoritative or commanding, his voice tone makes it impossible. It was for this reason that early in his career he was cast as an ineffective authority figure. His voice is incongruous with his body and actions. Paul Lynde used this incongruity as the basis for a comic figure he created. You should be aware of the tone of your voice and its ability to emphasize certain actions. The actions you select should be consistent with your voice.

MONOLOGUE EXERCISE

Freedom of body movement is an important part of complete expression. There are a number of different exercises I use to enable students to at least feel what a free body is like. But before trying those exercises, read the monologue below, from Edmond Rostand's classic drama of heroic romance, *Cyrano de Bergerac*. This is your first opportunity to act and be free; you're going to be an actor for this preliminary exercise. Read the monologue silently, then perform it with your body. No words yet—use the vocabulary of your body. Stand in front of a mirror and perform the actions Cyrano describes. Be free. Let your hands swing through the air. When he uses the word "creep," you creep. Don't worry about illustrating every word—that's charades—just put the spirit of the words in motion. (Possible actions are parenthesized.)

CYRANO: (*Challenge*) What would you have me do?
   Seek for the patronage of some great man, and like
   a creeping vine on a tall tree
Crawl upward where I cannot stand alone?
No thank you! (*Mock*) Dedicate, as others do, Poems to
   pawnbrokers?
Be a buffoon, in the vile hope of teasing out a smile on
   some cold face?
No thank you! (*Intimidate*) Eat a toad for breakfast ev-

ery morning? Make my knees callous and cultivate a
supple spine—
Wear out my belly groveling in the dust? No thank
you!
(Defy) Scratch the back of any swine that roots up gold
for me? Tickle the horns of Mammon with my left
hand while my right, too proud to know his partner's
business, takes in the fee? No thank you! *(Inspire)*
Use the fire God gave me to burn incense all day long
under the nose of wood and stone?
No thank you! *(Demean)* Shall I go leaping into ladies'
laps and licking fingers?
Or—to change the form—navigate with madrigals for
oars, my sails full of the sighs of dowagers? No thank
you!

The Cyrano monologue is a good one to return to from
time to time to check your progress in gaining freedom of
movement. As you feel more comfortable with your body,
your movements will become more expansive and you will
have more fun with the monlogue.

To gain freedom of body movement, use these exercises.
Again, they should be fun. For each of them it is necessary
to begin by making a personalization. By now you should
know how to do this: select a person who you have feeling
for, preferably someone who has hurt or angered you. Actually imagine that person sitting in a chair in front of you.
Keeping that person clearly in your mind, give yourself an
intention. It may be to criticize, accost, challenge, or attack, but it should be an action you were incapable of taking in real life.

PELVIC AGGRESSION

Begin talking to the person you have selected. Tell them
what you were never able to tell them before. Feel the emo-

tions start to twist inside you. Now, as you talk, emphasize each point you make by thrusting out your pelvic area. This is the old bump-and-grind. "I want you to listen to me!" *Bump!* "You never paid any attention to me!" *Bump!* If you can't get that quite right, pretend you've got a hula hoop around your waist. As you're confronting this person, twist your hips to keep the hula hoop twirling. Have fun as you do this. Enjoy the freedom of movement you're experiencing.

SEXUAL TENNIS

Later, when you are confident enough to make personalizations with someone else, this exercise becomes "sexual tennis." Stand a few feet apart and confront each other with your chosen intention. But as you do that, imagine that you are trying to bounce a ball back and forth and can only use your hips and pelvic area to do so. Push out with your pelvic area—thrust out hard. Don't forget your intention, but keep the ball bouncing.

There are a number of alternative exercises you can utilize to accomplish the same purpose, to free the body by introducing new movements. The first of these I have imaginatively named:

"MAKING A PIZZA"

It involves no cooking. Create a personalization and begin expressing your intention. Tell this person off. And, while you are aggressively accosting, challenging, attacking, or pleading with this person, put your body to work making an imaginary pizza. The movements should be fun. Stretch the dough. Pull it. Flip it up into the air. Get mad at this person and throw chunks of dough at him. Be active, alive, animate. You are using the pizza just as you used numbers when learning to make personalizations, as a substitute for your own natural movements. Eventually your body will take over and express the meaning of the words at the same time you are saying them to this imaginary person. The body knows this language. Nature equipped it with that knowledge. But, like someone who once knew French and forgot it because they didn't use it, the body has to be reintroduced to free movement. We are not trying to train your body to take new actions, rather to let it relearn something that has been prohibited.

PLAYING THE PIANO

This is an alternative motion exercise. As you make your personalization, instead of kneading and throwing the pizza dough, imagine an entire piano keyboard in front of you. Play the proper music to go with the feelings you are trying to express. If you're angry, really bang down on the keyboard. Use your fingers—get them moving again. Use the entire keyboard. Run scales. Swing your arms through the air. Eventually, all of these actions will become words.

ANIMAL EXERCISE

A final set of alternative exercises are simply animal impersonations. Often we admire people and try to copy their particular style. This is difficult, because the moment they realize they are being studied, they behave differently. Observe an animal, any animal, a cat, a dog, a bear, a goldfish, a bird. You can observe the animal as closely as possible, and it will not behave differently. Try to see how the animal moves. Study its musculature, the attitude it takes, the body posture. Doing this will help sharpen your ability to pick up character traits. Once you have studied the animal, imitate its movements.

Get down on all fours if you are acting the movement of a

cat or dog. Crawl on your stomach if it is a snake. Try to feel the essence of the animal. Attempting this particular exercise will force you to break old patterns of movement. Stretch and roll and crawl and perform all the different movements the animal you selected does. Imitate that animal as closely as possible. "Become" the animal.

Your body remembers. It has an entire vocabulary stored inside, just waiting to be released. In the words of Ralph Waldo Emerson: "Do not say things. What you are stands over you the while, and thunders, so I cannot hear what you say to the contrary."

CHAPTER SIX:
Character—Fashioning the Action

It is circumstance and proper measure that give an action its character.

—PLUTARCH

Imagine a cookie jar filled with the most delicious cookies ever baked. There is only a single batch, so the jar is guarded. But these cookies are so good everyone wants them and will use any means to get them.

John Wayne might stride manfully into the kitchen, his six-shooters dangling at his side, and say commandingly, "Ma'am, those are about the best cookies I've ever seen, and I'm afraid I'm gonna have to take 'em from ya. My father fought for those cookies. They rightfully belong to my family." He would walk forward and take the cookies.

Raquel Welch, dressed in something tight and suggestive, might march purposefully into the kitchen and, dazzling the guard with her appearance, explain, "You don't think you're going to let me have the cookies, do you? You don't understand at all. You never did. It's important to me that I have them. And," she would finish, lightly touching his cheek, "I don't think you want to stop me from taking them, do you?"

Woody Allen would stomp defiantly into the kitchen and go directly to the cookie jar. He would open it with a snarl, get his hand stuck inside, and end up smashing it on the floor. The guard would be laughing so hard that Woody would scoop up an armful of cookies and scamper away.

Mary Tyler Moore would walk in with her eyes wide and innocent. On the verge of tears, she would unfold this terrible tale of tragedy to the guard and make him want to put his arms around her and support her. Without even realizing it, he would give her the cookies to make her happy.

Peter Lorre would open his bug eyes, smile in a slightly crazed manner, and warn, "If you do not give me all the cookies, then I will have to blow up this kitchen and all the people in it. I don't want to, but I must. You do understand, don't you?"

Carol Burnett would trip over the doorstep and fall into the room. Getting up, she would slip again, arms and legs askew, reaching out to the guard for help. When he bent over to help her, she would pull him down and they would get tangled. Eventually, just to get her out of the kitchen, and out of his sight, he would demand she take the cookie jar and leave.

Robert Blake would just take the cookies. Not only that, he would probably take the recipe, too.

The point is, each person would go after those cookies in his own particular manner. By being aware of the type of actions that work best for them, they would know precisely how to get the cookies. Each of us also has a particular manner, a way of taking actions that is ours alone. It is our trademark, and is known as our character.

You are unique. There is no one else exactly like you. Other people might look like you, or sound like you, or even act somewhat like you, but no one puts the whole package together in precisely the same fashion. It is your character that makes you an individual.

Character is the result of bringing all your parts together. The way in which you reveal or disguise your emotions and thoughts, through speech and movement, is the way you show your character. It is not so much what actions you take, rather how you take them. It is the manner in which you use your voice, your body, your intelligence and emotions to achieve your goals.

Your character can be broken down into specifics—your characteristics. A characteristic may be the particular tone of your voice, certain word choices you make, an unusual way of taking a simple action, a nervous habit, or a special way of using your hands. These are the fingerprints of your personality, and lumped together, they form your character.

Use your imagination again. This is a game more than an exercise. This time, imagine you are a professional impersonator. You now have a wonderful ability to imitate voices. Your body is free and supple and you can recreate postures and movements. Like every other impersonator, you bring famous people "to life" by picking out their mannerisms, or characteristics, and broadly recreating them. Certain people are easy to impersonate. To do Ed Sullivan, you suck in your cheeks, clasp your hands behind your back, and welcome everyone to "a really big shew." Alfred Hitchcock is also easy—just stick out your stomach, puff up your cheeks, and speak in a slow, mournful voice with an English accent.

In doing your act, what characteristics of Barbra Streisand would you pick out to imitate? Her nasal voice? Her Brooklyn accent? Which mannerisms would you select to make your audience "see" Elvis Presley? Carroll O'Connor as "Archie Bunker"? Pearl Bailey? Barbara Walters? Truman Capote?

Finally the toughest of all. How would you "do" yourself? What characteristics would you broadly imitate that would make this impersonation recognizable to your family and friends? Your unusual voice? The way you use your hands? The unusual manner in which you hike up your shoulders when you walk? That particular way you frown when you're unhappy. Think about it.

You may not even know where to begin. You may have no idea how other people perceive you. Invariably, when someone hears himself on a tape recorder for the first time he responds by claiming, "That's not me. The other person sounds exactly like *you*, but that isn't *my* voice." Or, upon seeing a photograph of himself, "That's awful. Do I look like that? I don't look like that? Do I?"

You probably have a good idea of what you look like, but can you imagine how you look walking down the street? Or using your face to emphasize a point? Or how other people see you while you're working? Incredible as it may seem, you're probably more aware of the characteristics of your favorite performer than you are of your own mannerisms. You may hardly be aware of your very unusual, very particular, and very personal character.

The following exchange with a student in class is an example of the struggle for character identity:

WARREN: What do you feel like you want to do tonight in these exercises, Brad?

BRAD: *(Clutches his stomach)* I still want to get that out of there, you know.

WARREN: What do you think it is?

BRAD: It's a lot of things. It's insecurity. It's lack of self-esteem. *(Verge of tears)*

WARREN: Yes. Tell me about that. It's what? Try to get it out.

BRAD: I think it's just wanting to be somebody. Wanting to do something.

WARREN: I think that's exactly what it is. In other words, you want to do something so that you'll have a chance to be somebody. A lot of people judge their worth by what they do. Yes, some man does not make the football team, and so he spends the rest of his life . . . *[Brad angrily punches out . . . bends forward and lets go]* . . . but just as soon as they accomplish something, then they're very valuable!

In other words, if you made a film, they would love you, when they would *really* love the character, but you would feel they loved *you*. There's so much of your value involved in your accomplishment that you cannot accomplish.

You are valuable whether you can act or not. You're not valuable in some ways, box-office–wise, but as a human being, you're valuable. You're putting your head on a chopping block every time you do a scene . . . and it's pretty hard to work with that kind of pressure. I know people who are very successful who are much more miserable than people who have no success at all. The successful cannot talk to you without telling you something important that they're doing. You can never meet the person, you only meet their anxiety and their fears. When you act from that kind of disposition, you can work, but it's never meaningful.

You have made much progress in the fact that you've made a change in a very short time. You're changing in that you're getting close to yourself . . . then you'll have potential. But you keep contrasting yourself against types. A lot of people do that. "I must be that type . . . no I'm really that type." Sometimes they change their type three or four times a day. The one thing you want to do as an actor is to *not* remind anyone of anyone. Cary Grant, Marlon Brando have an identity all their own, and we contrast others against *them*.

How do you feel right now?

BRAD: I feel like I've gone back inside. I'm hiding down there—yes.

WARREN: I want you to say some adjectives you'd like us to see in you.

By the way, some very dynamic actors on the screen are

very dull people in real life. I want to hear the adjectives you really want us to see in you.

BRAD: Intelligent. Masculine.

WARREN: That's the one we all want. I'm sure if Don Knotts was really honest . . . *(Brad laughs)*

BRAD: Clever. Successful. Masculine.

WARREN: Now, let me ask you. Can you name me somebody who has these qualities that I would know? Jack Nicholson? Someone else? Now, don't cheat.

BRAD: *(Almost inaudible)* Robert Redford.

WARREN: Why should you avoid saying Robert Redford? You do look intelligent. You do not look dumb and stupid at all. You look masculine.

BRAD: I know I look intelligent.

WARREN: Is there someone you're around who has made you feel you're not particularly bright?

BRAD: Well, yes. Yes, sure, but I'm not so much around them as under them.

WARREN: The first time I saw Robert Redford was in a play, ten or fifteen years ago. He was almost pretty! He had a very pretty face, not very rugged at all. He was sort of a Hollywood pretty boy. Then when I saw him again in *Butch Cassidy and the Sundance Kid*, his face had gotten just enough disturbance. Something in him had matured. It gave the impression of his having been through the school of hard knocks. Tony Curtis, Robert Wagner, they were very pretty men. Actors go through different stages in their careers. Someone like Tab Hunter . . . he also had a pretty face like the others, but his lifestyle never allowed evident maturity. He never acquired the facial maturity of Redford. When maturity came for Robert, it put him in another category. Most of your insecurities are imagined. You have been playing a role for someone else. You've been acting less forceful than you are, less attractive, less intelligent. Most people are cast in the same role for the rest of their lives.

BRAD: I don't know if it's right, but for the last few days,

I've been going along discovering that I know the road you're talking about, I'm discovering it, and I feel like maybe I should take a role for myself, in life, like not smile so often . . .

WARREN: Nothing wrong with playing a role, as long as the role is not playing you.

On a blank piece of paper number from one to ten. Next to each number write down a particular characteristic of yours. Don't be judgmental—it makes no difference whether it is good or bad—just list as many as you can remember. You probably will not be able to fill out the list immediately. Over the next few days, bring your attention to yourself, to your own special way of doing things, and try to complete the list. This will force you to become aware of aspects of your character, and will be very important in trying to make changes in your life.

Like the residents of Archer City, Texas, most of us fall into character types, or roles, in our relationships. You may be the leading player in one person's life, but a bit player in another's. Depending on the situation, you may play the heavy, the best buddy, plain roommate, sex symbol, wise elder statesman, funny sidekick, or ingenue. By becoming aware of your character, you will begin to see what kind of behavior works best for you in each relationship. This knowledge will enable you to be more specific in choosing actions that will help you get exactly what you desire.

Different people act differently. They may have the same goal in mind, but each will try a different method to achieve it. Don Knotts, for example, would take very different actions than Robert Mitchum. Mitchum is probably most effective taking forceful, commanding actions, while Knotts would increase his chances for success by utilizing the strongest aspect of his character, his ability to be humorous. If he tried seriously to take the same forceful actions as Mitchum, he would have less chance for success.

Understanding your character will enable you to work with it. Once you learn which of your characteristics are effective, attractive, or appealing, and which are less successful, you can be much more selective in your actions. You can choose the specific actions which will work for you. One of Cher's most attractive features is her hair, and she knows how to emphasize it by carelessly tossing it over her shoulder. This attention-getting device makes her appear feminine and alluring. She understands how to use it for effect.

What is your most outstanding positive physical characteristic? How do you use it for effect? What actions do you take that emphasize this characteristic? If you're like most people, your answer will be, "Well . . ." Achieving your objectives requires that you use everything possible—and that includes your characteristics. If, for example, your voice is deep and resonant and exudes maturity, sophistication, and confidence, the telephone should be used to conduct business whenever possible. Or, if you are attractive, then emphasize your appearance. This doesn't mean you're getting by on your looks, which is a real fear many people have, but rather that you're using them in conjunction with your emotions and mind to achieve your objective. It means you are using all of your capabilities to the utmost.

Awareness of your character allows you to understand the type of behavior that is expected of you, and turn that to your advantage. There are a number of universal cliches. Meek people are not expected to take strong stands. Attractive women are not expected to be intelligent. Women are not supposed to be knowledgeable in business, or willing to take control and responsibility for major decisions. Men, in general, are not expected to show emotion in public. You have established a certain character, based on your behavior, in other people's minds. There is an established range of actions they expect from you. When you begin to take actions different from the norm; when you suddenly stand up for yourself, or show emotion, or take command, or allow yourself to express an opinion, you will immediately attract the attention of your supporting characters. They will suddenly be forced to deal with you in a new way. They will no longer be sure what actions will work to their advantage. But you can't take any steps to act out of character until you fully understand your own character and how other people perceive you.

That would be a relatively simple task if you could observe yourself from another person's point of view. The next best thing is to bring your full attention to your actions and the way you attempt them. Once you understand your character, you will be amazed at your ability to attract attention by taking actions different from those normally expected of you. The fine young actor Burt Young used his awareness of his character to turn a bit part into a springboard for a tremendous career. Burt is heavy, very tough, and not a glamour boy. In *Cinderella Liberty* he played the cliché role of a veteran Navy bosun's mate. His "big" scene required him to refuse James Caan's request for a leave. Normally a character of this type would sit behind a desk doing paperwork. Burt did the unexpected, he made the character vain. He turned down Caan while standing in front of a mirror combing his receding hairline and putting on cologne. He was noticed, and remembered.

The unexpected action must not be totally unsuitable, however. The history of movie comedy, from Charlie Chaplin to Lily Tomlin, includes countless stories based on the misadventures of a character who attempts to take actions unsuited to him. In Woody Allen's play-movie *Play It Again, Sam*, a shy, clumsy, physically slight character tries to become socially successful by taking actions suggested to him by the ghost of Humphrey Bogart. The result is hilarious failure.

One of the primary reasons people attempt the wrong actions is that they don't see themselves as they really are. Instead, they believe themselves to be a person they once were, or would like to be. I frequently see naturally attractive women using layers of makeup trying to make themselves attractive. They don't realize that they already are appealing. Adults who were fat children often see themselves as overweight, and continue to move, dress, and take actions as if they were still carrying that extra weight.

One of my students was tall and stately, with large features. For some reason, she thought of herself as a cute, sweet, ingenue type. A woman this size normally has a deep, mature voice, but she spoke in placating, high tones. Instead of using her impressive size to her advantage by choosing commanding or imposing actions, she was meek and ingratiating. The first thing I brought to her attention was that she was never going to be Debbie Reynolds. She simply wasn't the cutesy type and never would be.

That came as a shock to her. Her life and career weren't going anywhere, I explained, because she thought and acted like a gentle hummingbird, instead of thinking that she had a charging rhino inside. If she would release that charging rhino, it would probably take her anywhere she wanted to go. In class I gave her exercises that would force her to be commanding or dominating. I let her rehearse for life through these exercises. She began to use her full voice and eventually began speaking with her whole body. After almost eight months of work, she charged down to WNBC and emerged with her own daily segment on a news show. She got this job because she learned to speak with the authority her presence demanded.

Many people discovered certain actions that worked for them early in life and refused to change them as they grew, even though those actions were no longer effective. Many children gain attention and friends, for example, by telling jokes and wisecracking. They continue this behavior as they mature, and often end up being criticized for their loud, boorish ways. People, as well as actors, outgrow certain roles. Performers have agents to tell them that they can no longer be successful in a certain part, but you have only yourself. You must be able to take a good look at yourself as you really are. That list of ten characteristics you made should be kept and periodically changed to reflect changes you make in your characteristics. It should be a reminder to continually examine the way you behave and how that behavior translates into specific actions.

How did you get to be the person you are? Where did characteristic number six begin? Very possibly during your childhood. Many characteristics develop as protection for the emotions. Attempting to draw attention away from our emotions, we often build up other areas. Alan Finestein, a television veteran featured in *Looking For Mr. Goodbar*, is a sensitive person who was probably extremely delicate as a child. To protect his emotions, he built up his body, literally constructing a fortress. He even exercised and could control his facial muscles. When I started working with him, his physical appearance formed the overwhelming part of his character. Gradually, as he became more confident in his ability to deal with real feelings, he lost about fifty pounds, his face loosened up, and he exposed his sensitive character to the world. As he became comfortable with the person he really was, his whole character changed.

Many young women use their bodies the same way he used his muscles, to draw attention away from their emotions. Often women who are extremely sensitive and fragile concentrate on what I call the T-verbs; they titilate, torment, tease, and tantalize, the absolute musts for a sensuous woman. Of course, it is a dodge. Marilyn Monroe is the ultimate example, but I saw this same characteristic in Susan Blakely. She was a very successful model before she began studying with me, but had not worked a lot as an actress. The first problem I encountered working with her was simply getting her to be still. She would stand on the stage and her eyes would dart around the room, her hands would fidget, her legs would be constantly shifting. If you looked at the total picture, she appeared to be a playful beautiful girl. But then I saw that she shut her eyes tight whenever she laughed. When she was secure enough to stand still and open her eyes, I saw that behind much of her laughter was pain. She had learned to close her eyes to what she was really feeling and carry on through laughter. As I learned from watching Marilyn Monroe, some of her body behavior that seemed so alluring was really evasive. It was movement to avoid being hurt. Susie used her appearance to lead people away from what was really going on inside. It was her body language. It helped make her a successful model, but limited her as an actress. She was afraid to reveal the mature, emotional side of her nature. After working through much of this using the exercises, she not only had access to the capricious, playful behavior, but also the serious, mature woman behind it.

Other people pick up specific characteristics through childhood trauma. One of my students could not use her right hand while she was performing. She could not take any action involving her right hand. We discovered during a personalization that she had never been permitted to confront or disagree with her mother. In her mind, her mother was a saint, an image her mother fostered, although the woman was really very human and did very human things. Believing her mother was perfect, she thought of herself as a bad person anytime she did something to displease her. Even when she was punished, her mother was right because she was teaching her child how to be a good person. This student had never been permitted to act out any anger. As a result, she turned all her anger inward.

She wanted to strike out against her mother with her right hand, but knew it was wrong, so the hand became frozen. This was an obvious aspect of her character. During one exercise I made her bring all of her attention to that hand, and it began to tremble. I told her to pick up an imaginary object in that hand. She chose a knife. When I told her to allow the hand to do whatever it wanted to, she began ripping herself apart with this imaginary knife. This was one of the most frightening things I have ever seen. I stopped her and told her to let the hand do what it really wanted to do.

She turned it out on her mother. She just cut her mother up, finally releasing the anger that had created great tension and anxiety, robbed her of the use of her emotions, and restricted the use of her right hand. Once she was able to face her mother, through these personalizations, she recovered use of that hand and began to move freely and easily once more.

Some characteristics are the result of physical problems. The great romantic hero, Rudolph Valentino, was known for his dark, brooding eyes. The wife of Harry Cohn, former head of Columbia Pictures told me she and her husband had once taken a boat trip with Valentino. At dinner he had been charming and friendly, but later, when he passed her in a passageway, he ignored her. He was completely aloof. When she told her husband, he immediately confronted Valentino.

The star apologized, then explained that he was nearsighted, almost myopic. What the world perceived to be a sexy characteristic, a look that men desperately tried to imitate, was nothing more than a case of bad vision. If Valentino had not squinted, he probably could not have seen the face of the girl he was kissing.

Other characteristics happen naturally. President Franklin Roosevelt always turned the brim of his hat back in a jaunty manner. The reason had nothing to do with self-confidence. He was not able to put a cigarette to his lips, so he used a long cigarette holder. He had to turn the brim of his hat up so he wouldn't burn it.

Habits, methods of releasing tension, can also become characteristics. One of my students had long hair that she was constantly twirling around her fingers. When she decided to change her appearance, as part of breaking established character patterns, she had her hair cut short. The next time I saw her she was, without thinking, twirling imaginary strands of hair. She was actually waving her fingers through the air.

How do you determine exactly what type of character you've developed and which actions will work best for you? The key to utilizing your character is knowing precisely what it is. That self-knowledge will prevent you from becoming a hummingbird in a rhino's body. Examine the list you are compiling. It should tell you much about the way you take actions in the everyday world. This close examination is exactly what most people do not do. It is a matter of bringing awareness to each part of yourself as you perform an action.

Know thyself. Know how you take an action. While you are taking that action, observe how you attempt to charm or command; how you move; how you either do or do not use objects or "props" available to you; how you utilize your costume, the clothes you wear, to aid in the completion of an action. Listen to the sound of your own voice. Try to feel your hands as they move. Identify the emotion you're feeling. The object is to try to see yourself as others see you.

Bring the same observation to yourself that you brought to the animal exercises. Just as you practiced watching animals, observe yourself. Look for the obvious first. How are you sitting? Or standing? Do you bounce when you walk? Do you speak with your hands? Are you conveying any emotion through your voice or body? Do you maintain eye contact with the person you're talking to?

It is important to remember that you are not judging your character. You're making yourself aware of the way you do things, so you can discover if you are doing them in the best possible way. Your object is to determine which of your characteristics are beneficial, and which are not. This requires bringing your attention to yourself as you go through the day.

A good way to begin examining your character is to take a look at yourself in the mirror. The reflection you'll see is the appearance you present. The physical part of your character is extremely important to know when selecting actions. Consider your size, posture, and appearance and make sure they are in agreement with the type of actions you choose. Big people should attempt actions to dominate. Meek actions do not work as well for big people. Smaller people might try to entice or intrigue, as commanding actions will not be as successful for them. Other people are aware of your appearance. Because of their experiences, they will immediately cast you as a certain type. You can either take advantage of that, by taking actions consistent with that casting, or try to break out of it. Breaking out of it will be more difficult. Knowing you are being cast will not limit you to actions appropriate to your particular physical type, but you will find that these actions will generally be more effective.

If after making your list of characteristics and examining your physical appearance, you find that some or all of these character traits are not effective for you, it is quite possible to make major changes. That is the whole purpose of this book. Remember, just as an actor can play different roles, you can make changes in your character. This is not a matter of role playing; it is a method of finding the actions that will enable you to achieve your objectives. Throughout your entire life, you may well have been playing a role someone else created for you, a character totally unsuited to you. You may have been type cast at an early age and never been able to break out from that role. By analyzing your character—what you really are—you should be able to discover the proper role for yourself and the best actions to take in that role.

You are not born one way and destined to live that way throughout your life. Some people refuse to believe that. They are afraid to change anything about themselves. They won't even wear a new type of clothing unless someone whose opinion they respect gives them permission. They are trapped. You must allow yourself to be open to change. If you are not happy with the role you are playing, change is the only way out. Start small. Cut your hair or let it grow. Change your makeup; grow a mustache. Start using your hands when you speak. Wear a hat. Carry an umbrella, a walking stick, a pipe, something out of your normal "character." Small changes will lead to bigger ones.

By the reaction you receive from your supporting cast, "You've lost weight," "I like your mustache," "Where'd you get your hair cut?" you'll see that other people will notice changes you make and usually begin to take slightly different actions toward you. They will reestablish your character part in their minds.

In order to make change worthwhile, you must discover which changes are effective and which are not. Often this is a matter of trial and error. You must take new actions and observe how well they work. Among the things you might try, to see how new actions can cause changes, are:

1. During your next conversation, make a conscious effort to take one specific type of action. Be commanding. Try to gain sympathy. But every movement, every sentence, the way you use the environment (see Chapter Nine) should be consistent with the action you choose.

2. Women should wear their hair very differently than they do now. If you wear it up, let it fall free; if you normally let it hang, tie it up. Men should part their hair differently than they are currently doing, if possible.

3. Carry a prop. This can be anything that you normally do not carry.

4. Be aware of the tone of your voice. Try to speak easily

and comfortably, try to remove any strident tone from your voice.

5. Use your hands in a descriptive fashion as you speak.

6. When you have a clear-cut objective involving a number of different people, use a different action with each person to try to achieve the same objective. Again, be consistent in each action, and be aware of the result.

7. Smile broadly in a normal work situation and be aware of the reaction you receive from other people.

How do you choose other changes? Many people imitate the character of someone they admire. The theory is simple, if it works for another person there is no reason it shouldn't work for me. You want the cookies, and you observe Robert Blake just walk into the kitchen and take them. So you begin taking actions that work for Robert Blake. And, for some people, it might work. They'll get the cookies, the love, or the money, but for most people it won't. Everything an actor like Robert Blake does is consistent with his character. They way he walks, talks, and thinks is his own style. Picking up some of his actions probably won't work for you, and copying all his actions isn't possible.

I saw this imitative process at work at the Actor's Studio. At the time, James Dean and Marlon Brando were the biggest stars and everyone wanted to imitate their success. Both men were subjective, introverted, introspective, nonverbal, extremely private people. But this was consistent with their characters. Suddenly, though, slender boy-next-door basketball players from Indiana would come into class dressed in the prerequisite torn T-shirts and combat boots, tense their upper lips, stare at the floor or ceiling when they spoke, and hunch their shoulders. If they had tried to play basketball that way, they would have ended up rolling the ball down the court.

In everyday life Marlon Brando has what is called verbal tension, his upper lip gets tense when he speaks. The young actors, seeing that it worked for him, tried to imitate his manner of speaking. They ended up trying to be inarticulate to succeed, in a profession that requires articulation, instead of discovering what their strongest character aspects were and working to magnify them.

There is nothing wrong with observing someone you admire and trying to understand what makes him or her effective, and then trying to adapt some of these actions to your own character. But you must adapt them, not imitate them. You must make them right for yourself, and then observe carefully to find out if they work for you.

You may, for example, work with someone who is extremely effective. Try to categorize their actions. See if they attempt different actions with different people or maintain one consistent character. Observe which aspects of their character they emphasize. Do they use their appearance to establish position? Do they dress in such a way as to draw attention to themselves? Are they unusually efficient? Always agreeable? Willing to create friction to make a point when they know they are right? If you feel it is necessary, start a list of their outstanding characteristics. This will allow you to see how they are effective. Then attempt the same actions, adapted to your own character.

The same method can be used to observe someone who is successful socially. Pay close attention to them and observe the actions they attempt and the results they achieve. Write these down, if necessary. Eventually patterns will emerge which will show you how this person is effective.

A good actor tries to create a new character every time he works. He tries to learn how this character would speak, move, and think. If his performance is successful, he becomes that character on stage. In fact, actors often develop mannerisms for certain roles and find they can't drop them after the role is completed. Actress Joan Hackett began smoking while making *Night Watch*, for example, and had great difficulty quitting once the show's run ended.

Actors create characters in much the same way you will examine your own character. First they learn as much as possible about their own instruments so they can determine what changes are necessary. Then they observe people similiar to the character they will be portraying, not only to select characteristics, but to see when these mannerisms come into play. Then they try to incorporate these actions into a character. They can determine how successful they are by the reaction of the audience. Your own success is dependent upon the achievement of your objective. If you achieve your goal, the actions you selected were correct. If you fail, they were the wrong actions.

Your next exercise is to attempt an actual change in your character. Observe someone who is successful at a task a number of times, if possible. Pick out one characteristic of theirs that you find appealing. Then incorporate it into your own character. The actual characteristic is not important. It may be the action they choose, the way they put it into effect, or a mannerism. It may be something as basic as always carrying a sterling silver pen and using it to emphasize a point. It is not even important that this characteristic work for you. The observation, analysis, and incorporation into your own character is what you are trying to experience.

The most elaborate characterization I ever created was of the great humorist Will Rogers. Strangely enough, even though I came from the Southwest, I knew very little about him. But while I was working on Broadway, in *The World of Susie Wong*, another cast member mentioned that my voice was reminiscent of Rogers'. Months later, while walking in Greenwich Village, I saw a Rogers biography in a bookstore and bought it.

After reading the book, I decided to try to recreate the

character as an acting exercise. My goal was to eventually write a one-man show, much like Hal Holbrook's *Mark Twain*. To do that I had to become Will Rogers.

I found some old records of his and listened to them incessantly, concentrating on his voice quality, his tone, and his speech patterns. Then I discovered some silent films he starred in and watched them for hours, studying his characteristics and movements. I picked up his small mannerisms. I knew when he would smile. I knew how he would smile. I stood in front of a mirror and learned how to take off a cowboy hat and scratch my head, just as he did. I practiced chewing gum, twirling a lasso, and twisting my cowboy hat in my hands.

I spent hours in front of a full-length mirror imitating his characteristics. I watched the movies and listened to the records. I analyzed his success and tried to recreate the aspects of his character that made him so universally popular.

One afternoon I was working on my makeup, trying to build up the beak of my nose, change my eyebrows, and comb my hair differently and a friend of mine walked in and discovered me. "You look just like Will Rogers," he laughed.

I told him my plan.

He stopped laughing. He worked as a publicity agent and had good connections with talent coordinators. "How'd you like to be on the 'Tonight Show?'"

"I just started," I explained. "I've never even done the whole act. I don't even have the material down pat yet."

He told me it didn't matter. I looked so much like Rogers and had his mannerisms down so well, I was sure to be a success. He convinced me to walk with him to the "Tonight Show" office in Rockefeller Center wearing my Rogers costume. I felt foolish but agreed, positive nothing could ever come of it.

Two nights later I was on the show. I still had never done a complete act. I'd never even tried stand-up comedy. Luckily, Johnny Carson had read the story in *Sports Illustrated* about my Army football career and brought me on stage out of costume to talk about that. It's a funny story and the audience responded pleasantly, so I had already established a rapport.

Author-humorist Harry Golden was also on the show that night, and he had actually known Rogers. Later, while I was backstage putting on my makeup and rehearsing my lines, he told Will Rogers stories. By the time I was introduced, the audience was so well primed it would have been difficult to fail. It all worked very well.

But what really made it work was an ingredient I could never rehearse. I was so nervous, so full of emotion, that the character actually came alive. Through my character I showed real emotion.

Later, when my schedule at the workshop made it impossible for me to continue the show I'd written, my material became the basis for James Whitmore's *Will Rogers*.

The point I am making is that, by observation, you can pick up effective traits and discard ineffective characteristics. You can become the cookie taker. Your physical appearance makes no difference as long as you select actions consistent with it. As long as the "how" is backed up by your voice, your body, your thoughts and feelings, all working toward the same goal, you can succeed.

You have been cast into a play. You may be playing the wrong role, but only you can determine that. Bring your attention to your character, see what aspects work for you, select new actions, incorporate them into your character, see how well they work for you, and in this way develop the role *you* want to be playing, rather than the role someone else has cast you into.

CHAPTER SEVEN:
Casting Call

Oh, wad some power that the giftie gie us
To see ourselves as others see us.

—ROBERT BURNS

TV COMEDY: Casting for Sharp NY Theatrical Agent type, 40–60; Seductive actress/dancer; Male-female soap opera types; Elderly Jewish tailor; Innocent male neurotic, 20's. Auditions . . .

STAGE CASTING: Cast breakdowns for *Broadway*: NICK VERDIS, middle-aged Greek, talks with dialect; LIL RICE, prima donna type, heavy and middle-aged; TOY LANE, slender, small-time song and dance; FIVE YOUNG CHORUS GIRLS; JOE, Italian waiter, dialect; BILLIE MOORE, beautiful chorus girl; DOLPH, dark, wiry man; PORKY, stout, balding; SCAR EDWARDS, slight, intense . . .

These advertisements are from *Backstage*, a weekly newspaper for professional actors. Besides news of the entertainment industry, it includes the lifeline of information for working performers—casting notices. Roles to be cast in plays, movies, or for television are annnounced and described. The description details the "type" of actor the producer is looking for. Professional actors know the types they are capable of playing, and when a notice is listed within their physical and performing range, they join the lines for an audition.

Part of the job for a working actor is knowing the type, or types, he is capable of portraying and working to develop his ability to perform that particular role, whether it be that of the icy executive or the carefree swashbuckler. Many actors work continuously, even though they may not be as gifted as other performers, because they have learned what their type is and have worked to develop strong characteristics for those roles.

I had been in New York only a short time when casting notices were posted for Tennessee Williams' *Sweet Bird of Youth*. One role to be cast was that of a young bartender with a southwestern accent. I was young. I was working as a bartender. I had a southwestern accent. So on a bitterly cold winter's morning I joined the long line of people standing outside waiting to audition for director Elia Kazan. When I finally reached the stage door, I was asked what agent sent me to the audition. The answer was no agent.

I was booted out of line.

Unwilling to give up, I went around to the front of the theatre and tried to talk that guard into letting me inside. "It's me," I carefully explained, "that part is me." He wanted no part in the making of a star and told me to beat it. Just as I was about to, his phone rang. Saved by the Bell system, I raced by him, into the theatre, up to the mezzanine, and beyond to the balcony, where I hid in darkness.

Kazan was alone in the audience and a steady stream of actors auditioned a few lines for him. I stayed in hiding for almost two hours. Then Kazan stood up and stretched and the single light on the stage was turned off. Summoning all my courage, I stood up and shouted, "Mr. Kazan! Mr. Kazan!"

Kazan ducked to the floor.

After a moment he raised his head and peered up into the blackness. "Who is that? Who's up there?"

I answered in a constricted voice. "It's Warren Robertson, Mr. Kazan."

Angrily, he ordered me down from the balcony. I hurried down to find myself standing face to face with one of the great Broadway directors. First he castigated me, then demanded to know what I was doing in the theatre.

I told him, in my best possible southwestern twang.

After listening to my story, and my accent, he thrust a script at me. "Okay," he said, "you can audition. But I'm telling you, this has nothing to do with your sneaking into the theatre. Don't let me ever hear about you doing something like that again. But you just happen to be the right type."

There are times in your life when nothing you do works the way you want it to. No matter how hard you try, you won't succeed. Perhaps you can't attract the person of your choice, or get the job you want, or aren't selected to represent your group. In many cases, you fail just because you are the wrong type. "They" want another "type" and no matter how hard you try, no matter how good you are, you simply aren't "right" for the person, or the job, or the convention. Recognizing that the world consists of people of varied types, that you are a specific type, and that other people typecast positions in business and social life can be vitally important. The first question you should ask yourself when dealing with another person is: What type are they looking for? Sophisticated? Casual? Businesslike? Personable? Physically attractive? By answering this question, you will be further able to choose actions that will be successful.

Everyone gets typecast. We all fit into one role more easily than any other. Your particular type isn't important, one "type" is not necessarily better than any other "type," but awareness that you are a certain type is essential.

Type is the larger category into which individual characters fit. Both Robert Redford and George Segal are leading man types, both of them are capable of playing comedy and adventure as well as romantic leads, but on screen they play very different types. If they were cast in the same role, they would play it very differently, they would play it to their own particular "type." Two accountants might be "cerebral types," meaning they use their intellects to solve problems, but when confronted with the same problem, each would use a personal method to find a solution. They are the same type, but they have different characters. Your type determines the range of actions which might prove effective for you. The way you carry out these actions is determined by your character.

Unfortunately, people tend to get typecast early in childhood. This emotional casting can last a lifetime. Many people spend their entire life acting as a childhood type that no longer exists. They utilize all the characteristics of this particular type. A fat little boy grows up to be a slim and attractive man, but retains the shy, withdrawn, and introverted behavior of the fat child. The once beautiful girl keeps all the mannerisms of her childhood—she remains true to type—no matter how much her appearance changes. The type you were cast into as a child is a difficult mold to smash.

Pause for a moment and remember the type of child you were. Try to identify yourself as you really were.

The realization that other people typecast you can be very helpful in achieving your goals. Your object should be to recognize the fact that certain actions will work better for your type than others, and to adopt those actions.

When your characteristics and appearance are wrong for

the actions you attempt, when you act out of type, the result is often exactly the opposite of what you intended.

Shawn Elliott, a student at the Workshop, played the lead in the New York production of *Jaques Brel Is Alive and Well and Living in Paris* and starred in the movie *Short Eyes*. He is tall, dark, and attractive. Among singers, he is much more the sexy Tom Jones or Sergio Franchi type than the cocky Frank Sinatra–Bobby Darin. But, as a child, because he *was* a child, he thought himself more in the Sinatra–Darin mold, and adopted the loose tie, jacket tossed casually over the shoulder, dangling cigarette, "I can make it on my own" mannerisms. Since he was tall, instead of projecting confidence to the audience, these actions made him appear conceited. He immediately turned off his audience. When I brought this to his attention he began changing. He allowed his type to develop naturally, taking advantage of the gifts he had, and developed a style much more suitable to his particular type.

Acting against type is one of the most destructive things a performer can do. People take up theatre wanting attention and acceptance for things they are incapable of doing in their real life. They imagine they can stand up on the stage and suddenly be transformed into a different and more desirable type. They will become Errol Flynn swashbuckling his way into your heart, or ooze the confidence of Katherine Hepburn. Because they are not these types at all, they only imitate the actions of real types and usually fail miserably.

The entire "B" movie industry grew up around imitation Clark Gables, Gary Grants, Joan Crawfords, and Carole Lombards. The reason most "B" actors never became stars is that they denied their own types. The few "B" players who successfully graduated into "A" pictures usually played a different type than they had in those earlier movies, a type much closer to their real selves. However, a lot of competent actors went to Boot Hill early trying to become "the next Gable," or "the new Brando," instead of "the original . . ."

In your life, acting against type can also cause problems. Instead of being able to bring all of your capabilities to an objective, you merely sputter along like a car with a worn-out engine.

The important thing to determine, before deciding if you are being true to type in your actions, is exactly what type you *are*. Remember what type you decided you were as a child; now from this list of celebrities, try to pick out the type closest to what you are now. This is much more complex than deciding who you most look like. Pick the people who you believe portray your type in their work:

John Wayne   Barbara Walters
James Stewart   Rita Moreno
Andy Griffith   Ted Knight
Burt Reynolds   Mary Tyler Moore
Robert Young   Sammy Davis Jr.
Pam Grier   Sylvester Stallone
Raquel Welch   Shelley Winters
Cicely Tyson   Woody Allen
Don Knotts   Jane Fonda
Don Rickles   Carol Burnett
Bea Arthur   Henry Fonda
Roy Scheider   Jimmy Brown
Farrah Fawcett-Majors   Mel Brooks
Goldie Hawn   Telly Savalas
George Kennedy   Jaqueline Bisset
Sidney Poitier

Were you able to categorize yourself as one of these people, or a combination of some of them? As you read this list, you probably recognized people who showed many of your character traits. It's also possible you didn't recognize your type on this list. That doesn't mean you can't be typed—

everyone is—but rather you are unsure precisely where you fit. Probably the easiest way to begin determining your type is to ask people that you know best, close friends or relatives, how they see you. They may be more aware of you than you are of yourself. They watch you closely, more closely than you examine yourself.

ESSENCE

You might also begin to understand how other people type you by playing a game called "Essence." It is not available in any store, costs nothing, and can be played with a group of any size. The object of the game is to identify a person by matching his type with specific objects. One player leaves the room and the remaining players select someone to be the subject. It may be another player or a well-known celebrity. When the first person reenters the room, each player describes the subject in terms of an object. "If that person were a car, it would be a . . . " and a specific car is named. "If that person were a movie, it would be . . . " and a specific movie is named. "If that person were food, it would be . . . " and a type of food is named. Using these clues, the first person tries to guess the identity of the subject.

How well do you know yourself? Now is an opportunity to really find out. Below is a list of objects. Try to find the specific type in each category that best matches yourself. Practice first. Select a movie star and try to type them through this list. If the object is a car, for example, David Niven might be a Rolls Royce, Jaqueline Bisset a Jaguar, Robert Blake a Ford pickup truck, and Nancy Walker a souped-up Volkswagen. If the subject was Robert Redford, you wouldn't match him with a Ford Maverick. The types don't match. This is not a value judgment: the car may be too good for him, or not good enough, but it certainly is not his type.

The types you should try matching yourself to are:

car	piece of clothing
television show	fruit
book	precious jewel
section of the newspaper	piece of furniture
color	fabric
country	US city
magazine	movie
denomination of money	other actor
wines	flower
breed of dog	song
sports team	

After completing this list, make a second list, using the same objects and match them with the type of person you'd like to be. The contrast between the way you presently see yourself and the way you'd like others to see you should prove fascinating. It would also be very helpful to get one or more of your friends to fill in this list for you. Using this list properly will help make you aware of your self-image as opposed to the way others see you. Knowing the image you project to the world is very important.

For many people this exercise will prove illuminating. They will see that they have outgrown their own image of themselves and will understand that they have little conception of the way other people see them.

Individuals who learn their own strongest type and take actions consistent with it, increase their chances for success. They achieve objectives because they take actions compatible with their type. But some people have no idea what their type is, or they consciously rebel against what they feel they really are, holding that self inside. These are the most common problems I see in my new students. Because understanding your type and how to use if for your own benefit is vital in the theatre, it is an important aspect of my work. Using the same basic exercises described in this book, I help students define their own type and work toward developing that type naturally and completely. Sometimes simply becoming aware that they constantly take the same type actions is enough to make a student either emphasize his particular type or take steps to change it. Other times much more work is needed to reach the roots that formed this character-type.

The wife of one of my students called me one day. The evening before he had tried to commit suicide. Although he failed, she knew he would try again until he was successful. Both his father and grandfather had taken their own lives. Observing this student, there was no way to tell that this incredible self-hatred existed. He was agreeable and placating—the docile sidekick type. He was so resigned to everything that happened to him, he simply stopped caring. Finally he became resigned to taking his own life, as his father and grandfather had.

He came into the workshop seeking some sort of escape from what he felt was his fate. Most of the scenes he rehearsed with other students involved him playing an aggressive, adventurous type—precisely the opposite of what he appeared to be in real life. At first I thought my job was to simply allow him to find his own type, but after that phone call I realized it was much more important that I give him a means to express the anger he was holding inside.

He had been seeing a psychiatrist and, obviously, that had not helped. In fact, I spoke to the psychiatrist. He explained that the student felt it absolutely necessary to protect his parents, even though they had disappointed him. As a child, he could not allow himself to get mad at his father, even though by taking his life his father had left him alone.

The doctor had tried conventional methods to deal with this student's problems, so I decided to try humor. Humor is one of the most effective weapons in the problem-solving arsenal. At that time, I knew I represented someone he had a great deal of respect for—an authority figure—which is why he continued to come to class. My objective was to get him enraged at me, to force him to turn his anger out at the world and express it. I chose actions that I knew would provoke him: taunting him, making fun of him, and making it obvious I was humoring him.

During the next class I called him up on stage for an exercise. Without letting him know I'd spoken to his wife, I steered the conversation toward death. "It looks to me like you're the type who wants to be shuffled off this mortal soil."

He admitted considering suicide. The class became absolutely still, understanding this was an extremely serious exchange. I asked him if he was just thinking about it, or had he actually started planning his suicide.

"Are you making fun of me?" he asked. I detected the slightest touch of anger in his voice.

"Yes, I am," I told him honestly. "In fact, the thought of you taking your life is one the most hilarious things I've ever heard. You'll have to pardon me if I want to laugh about it."

Instead of getting angry, he became very protective of his feelings. He froze. It was still impossible to get him angry. "You know," I continued, "the thought of you, an attractive young man in the prime of life, the sort of fine person you are, taking your life . . . I know it's ridiculous—it may even sound sick—but I find it funny."

He said nothing.

"I think we have to look at this realistically. You have a motorcycle, don't you?" He admitted he did. "Well, I don't have one, and I'd like one. And there are a few other things, some of the clothes you've worn to class are pretty nice and we're about the same size."

A few people in the class began laughing nervously. The student was being sucked into the discussion. "Are you kidding me?"

"Absolutely not. And another thing I'd like to do. I don't advertise my school. If you could give me some idea of your plan, I could be there. I could find you and then I could get the photographer from the *News,* and I'd be pointing toward your body. I can see the headlines: ACTING TEACHER FINDS BODY. I could get some good publicity out of it."

"Just stop it?" he asked me. He didn't tell me, he asked me.

"I'd like to light the whole thing if possible," I decided. "I can get the proper lighting and maybe we can add a little background music."

"Cut it out, huh?"

I kept going on like this and he kept warning me to stop.

"Maybe you could, you know, jump off a lighthouse. You'd land upside down in the sand and I know we'd get tremendous publicity . . . "

He started letting his anger go. He took small steps toward the front of the stage, almost as if he were trying to attack me. That was exactly what I wanted to see. I ordered him to stay right where he was and make a personalization.

Without a pause, he attacked his father. "You Goddam weak bastard, you son of a bitch, I had to grow up all alone as a child . . . " He started throwing out his arms, striking out at the memory of his father. He found words he had never been able to say. Of course, as soon as he realized he had allowed his anger to show, he retreated into the safe nice-guy type he had created as a child.

I knew I wouldn't have to worry about him for the next week. He would be back in class, if only to see if I had the audacity to ridicule him again.

Although I rarely give the same students exercises for two consecutive weeks, he was the first person I called up the following class. "I've been thinking about it," I started. "I think I have a better plan. We can make a movie about this! There's a little place I know upstate, right by a brook. It has a tree. I'd like to produce the whole show, if it's all right with you . . . " The class started to laugh, and even the student began chuckling. It was absurd.

But I kept prodding and he began to get angry again. I put two empty chairs side by side on stage and told him to imagine his parents were sitting in those chairs. "I want you to challenge your father," I told him. "I want you to defy him and dominate your mother." What I really wanted was to force him to express the emotions he was shepherding and direct them at the people who had molded him into a nice, always agreeable sidekick type, instead of the vibrant type he seemed to really be.

He exploded with anger at the two imaginary people, spewing out the intense pain that had immobilized him and caused him to give up on life for almost thirty years.

These emotional outbursts might well have saved his life. Using the emotional material he discovered in these exercises, he changed his type. While he was once docile, he often became pleasantly aggressive. He began fighting back, setting goals for himself to become the person he was capable of being. He is still working in the theatre and his whole life has changed. As an actor he is now capable of an entire new range of parts, and as a person he is able to control his own life.

There is no such thing as a good or bad type; there are different types. If you are going to fulfill your potential, you must become aware of the image you present to the world. You must understand how other people type you, and use that knowledge to your advantage.

How? People attribute certain characteristics to particular types. The nice-guy type will step aside. The studious type will not fight back. The beautiful woman will not be intelligent. The unattractive woman will not be feminine. These are clichés, but they have gained a foothold of acceptance. By taking those actions expected of your type, when it is to your advantage, you can eliminate many obstacles. Or, by going against type, you can immediately attract attention. The nice guy suddenly says no. The studious type becoming physical. The beautiful *and* intelligent woman. The sensuous unattractive woman. By going against expectations, each of these types can draw far more attention than would otherwise be possible. The key is to take advantage of that attention by using the right actions.

The more you work with your type, the easier it will be to discover what are the right actions, and what actions are not expected from you. If you work at this, one day you will select a specific action, with a specific objective in mind, and be totally aware of everything you do to take that action. The result will be as you intended. This awareness that specific actions can be selected based on your type will be a breakthrough. You'll begin to understand how to choose actions based on your own knowledge of yourself and the impressions of your supporting characters. You will begin to take control of your life.

By defining yourself as a specific type, in no way do you limit your possibilities. There are leading players of every type. No one can play to all audiences. In some of his movies, even Woody Allen gets the beautiful girl at the end. Just as different movies appeal to different people, there are different audiences for each type to play to.

Whichever type you are, it should be a rich, full statement of "I am." When it is not, when some of your parts are out of harmony, when you are busy being a type selected for you by someone else, a type you may be uncomfortable portraying, you hold yourself back. The nice man trying to be the aggressive-bold type is as ineffective as the strong woman trying to play the ingenue.

Your goal should not be to act like a type, but rather to discover how you are most comfortable. Once you know that, you can select your actions from that knowledge, and you will be able to bring your mind, body, and emotions to their successful completion.

CHAPTER EIGHT:
The Production Company ("Without Whom . . .")

And how, and who, what means,
And where they keep,
What company, at what expense,

—SHAKESPEARE

There really is no such thing as a one-man show. Even great one-performer shows, like Hal Holbrook's *Mark Twain Tonight*, Billy Dee Williams' *I Had a Dream*, and Lily Tomlin's *Appearing Nitely*, require the combined talents of many people, from producers to publicity agents, to make them successful. Your life is no different. To receive the best possible reviews, to get the most out of the material you have to work with, you need the full support of the entire cast of your play. Getting that support is often a difficult task.

If we lived alone, in a world in which we could be both performer and audience, it would be simple to make any changes we desired. If there was something we didn't like, or were not satisfied with, it would be easy to make the necessary changes without having to consider anyone else. But we don't live alone. We live in a world crowded by people who also have needs and desires, and whose objectives often conflict with ours. What is good for us may not be good for them. It is this supporting cast that makes real change difficult. Your success in dealing with them will ultimately determine how successful you will be in achieving your objectives.

SCENE: SUPPORTING CHARACTERS

In Herb Gardner's *A Thousand Clowns*, the stable, reliable brother Arnold explains to his iconoclastic brother Murray, "I finally figured out your problem. There's only one thing that really bothers you. Other people. If it wasn't for them other people, everything would be great, huh, Murray? . . . The Other People; taking up space, bumping into you, asking for things, making lines to wait on, taking cabs away from ya . . . The Enemy. Well, watch out, Murray, they're everywhere . . . "

The problem is, indeed, other people. They are everywhere. They have needs and desires and objectives just as you do. Their happiness is based on fulfilling their needs, and achieving their objectives, even if those goals are in direct conflict with yours.

It is human nature to care about other people. Everyone wants to be admired, appreciated, liked, or loved, and so we are careful about intentionally hurting other people's feelings. Often we allow this concern to control our lives, forgetting that the stronger and happier we are, the better all our relationships will be.

While one of your major objectives should be to improve the quality of the relationships you have with the supporting players in the cast of your life, it is vitally important to remember that these same people will do almost everything they can to make change difficult for you. Any change you make will affect each of your relationships. If, during the performance of a play, an actor changes a line or rehearsed action, the rest of the cast must respond to that change. The more substantial the change, the more the whole play will be altered. This makes the job of the other actors more difficult. It upsets the play as they have become accustomed to it. It may create small havoc or minor panic. This is just as true in your own life. Any change you make requires the people around you to react. It forces them to change, too.

And change can be very frightening to your supporting characters. People develop a lifestyle which enables them to cope with everyday life. They become so comfortable in this lifestyle, no matter how disorderly it might really be, that they accept it as order. Anything that threatens this security is to be both feared and fought.

Change threatens it. As a pebble landing in a calm pond sends out an endless series of ripples, any change you make in an established pattern is going to affect the whole pattern. The closer your relationship with someone else is, the more effect your changes will have upon their life. The greater the threat to their emotional safety, the harder they will fight to prevent your changing.

This has nothing to do with love or affection; this is survival. Most of us are limited in our actions more by the people we love and who love us than by our enemies. The most common method these supporting characters use to force us back into the familiar is emotional blackmail. They take full advantage of the feelings we have for them.

Since actions cause change, emotional blackmail is used primarily to prevent you from taking actions. It is a subtle technique, aimed at making you feel guilty or insecure. "It's all right," the long-suffering mother reassures her child, "go out and have a good time. I'll just sit here alone in front of the broken television set. I'm used to being left alone." The classic line of every borscht-belt comedian is, "Don't worry about me. The doctor said there was every chance I could still lead a useful life." The techniques are not always funny. Lines like, "If you do that, I won't love you anymore," or "How can you do that to me?" or "You're spending all your time on yourself. You don't have any time left over for me and the children. You don't love us anymore, but that's okay, we still love you," are intended to make you feel so guilty or insecure about the relationship that you will take no new actions. *He* or *she* wouldn't do it, but he or she is willing to suffer for you. Nothing could better promote guilt feelings. These are actions intended to intimidate you.

This technique is as effective as you allow it to be. The actions you take in response to these obstacles usually determine your ability to achieve your objective. When confronted by the intentions of your supporting characters, it is important to remember your own objectives and actions and to try to stick with them. If you allow yourself to be intimidated, you may save the relationship only at the expense of your own happiness. The other person will be safe—they will have achieved their objective at the expense of yours. Recognizing emotional blackmail as a common technique, used by everyone from spouse to employer, is the first step in meeting this conflict of objectives.

Sometimes the technique used by the blackmailer is not so subtle. I've seen a scenario regularly repeated in my classes. A married, shy, nonassertive woman, the type usually dominated by her husband, comes into class to begin studying. As she takes her first tentative steps toward becoming assertive and demonstrative, or as she begins to get excited about herself as a person and potential actress, problems begin to crop up in her marriage. Soon after, invariably, she becomes pregnant. I'll bet I've been responsible for more babies than the New York City blackouts.

The threat of change is responsible, of course. As soon as their docile wives begin to bloom and change, the buzzer of insecurity goes off in husbands. They first try to reason them out of change, but when that doesn't work, they tighten the chains with children. This is probably not even done consciously. Scared supporting characters simply use whatever weapons are at hand.

It happens in reverse occasionally, too. As soon as a man begins to think seriously about a career in theatre, or his career begins to blossom, or he begins to change, his wife becomes pregnant. The baby almost guarantees she'll keep him as he is, at least temporarily—precisely her objective.

Initiating real change in your life requires that you not only consider your own objectives, but that you also examine the objectives of those people who will be affected by your changes. What do they want out of life? What are they doing to achieve their goals? How are the actions you're planning going to conflict with their objectives? How will they react to the changes you initiate? Considering these questions is very important, because it will help you select the proper actions and make you aware of the true purpose of the emotional blackmailer.

There are a number of ways to win this battle of competing objectives. Most important, you must have a battle plan. This is nothing more than a clear understanding of your objective and how you intend to achieve it. How will you break it down into smaller intentions? What actions will you take? How will you carry them out? Once you have that knowledge, you will know when you are being sidetracked. Many people are enticed back into the old saddle without even being aware they've lost the battle.

Suppose you decide you need a better job with a higher salary. Finding this job is your objective. Your boss has no slot for you and is trying to keep the payroll down, but since you're a valuable employee he doesn't want to lose you. His objective is to keep you for the same salary. He might start

by attempting to make you feel guility. "I've taught you everything you know. I gave you your first chance. We really
need you here. I don't know what I'd do without you."

These are solid compliments designed to make you feel
like a rat for even thinking about leaving, but accompanied
by no pay hike or job change. If you allow yourself to be enticed, he will have accomplished his objective.

"All right," he continues, "I'll give you an extra fifteen
dollars a week. We can't afford it—you know business has
been bad—but I can't afford to lose you either."

It's not as much as you know you deserve, or desire, but
the boss has made it clear that he would be personally hurt
if you left. He probably wouldn't think very highly of you
either. If you accept his offer, you are still not achieving
your objective. The boss, using emotional blackmail, will
have won the battle.

Should you accept the offered compromise? Setting
specific goals for yourself will enable you to measure the
importance of the prospective change. The more specific
your objective, the less likely you will be to succumb to
blackmail. If you firmly decided that you wanted an additional fifty dollars a week and a promotion, a fifteen dollar
raise wouldn't be enough. However, if your objective was
simply an unspecified raise and promotion, you might be
tempted to take the offer.

Having specific goals will help you resist emotional pressure applied by people close to you. Suppose you refused the
fifteen dollar offer and your boss responded by turning red
and calling you an ingrate. Remember, this is a person
you've known, worked closely with, and liked for years.
Would you bow to his anger and accept the offer?

This is a tough decision. For many people the desire to be
liked and loved is so strong that they allow themselves to
be beaten back into place by the threat of withdrawal of
that affection. But when you start changing, you must be
willing to accept the responsibility for displeasing other

people. If you cannot do that, don't even consider attempting real changes in your life. You are admitting that you place other people's happiness before your own. You are admitting your life is out of your own control. Instead of becoming free to act, free to take whatever actions will benefit your life, you will continue to be dependent on the good will of your supporting characters.

There are a number of ways to fight emotional blackmailers. The first is to ignore them. Realize what they are doing, understand the consequences of your actions, and ignore the threats. Sometimes blackmailers will drop their demands and allow your intentions to take precedence. Other times, however, your independence may create a rift in your relationship.

A second way of dealing with emotional blackmail is to find new actions, or intentions, which will overwhelm the other person. Scream, yell, cry, ask for understanding, try to dominate, or explain that you are aware of exactly what they are attempting to do. Let the blackmailer know you are aware that they have an objective and do not intend to let it stand in your way. This action of yours to threaten or induce support may prove successful. In dealing with your supporting characters, you must be aware that a battle of competing intentions may have many rounds, and you have to be willing to adjust your actions to counter each action taken by the other person. You must meet their new actions with new actions of your own.

The most satisfying method to combat the blackmailer is to make him or her accept your change as beneficial rather than threatening. Try to choose actions to overcome their resistance by showing how they will gain. Prove that the changes will make your relationship more secure. Inspire them to aid you in making changes. This is not easy, but it can be done. A large segment of your supporting cast will be asking, "What's in it for me!" and you should try to provide the answer.

You may find it necessary to change your intentions many times in order to satisfy the demands of those people close to you. This is to be expected. Actors rehearse roles numerous times before finding precisely the right portrayal. You might have to try a dozen different intentions before discovering the one that works. It is worth experimenting, because change is much easier when you have the support of the people close to you.

Changing intentions until you find something that works may seem like manipulation. That is precisely what it is, but not of a negative sort. Manipulation is defined in the dictionary as, "to manage skillfully, sometimes to manage artfully." This is what I am urging you to do . My students occasionally accuse me of attempting to manipulate them. I explain that that is precisely what I am trying to do. "You're being manipulated with skill and finesse, and it's taken me fifteen years to learn how to do it, and you should be very happy that I can. Because if I couldn't, you would stay exactly where you are."

I am not suggesting that you deceive people, nor do anything that would harm another person. I use the term "manipulation" simply to imply taking an action with another person in mind. You have the ability to make your life what you want it to be, but to do that you must be able to manipulate the environment, instead of being subject to its manipulation.

Emotional blackmail is only one of the weapons your supporting characters might draw in their efforts to keep you in your role. If you seriously threaten their objectives, they may fight back with threats of their own. "If you want to continue your acting go ahead, but I'm going to leave you," or "If you continue to create problems with your demands for a raise, I'm going to have to let you go," or "I love you, but I can't be tied to one person. If it upsets you too much for me to see other people, maybe we should stop going out." You can either surrender to these attacks on your security, or respond by attempting new intentions that will satisfy their demands while keeping you moving toward your objective. To do this you must convince these other people that their objectives coincide with yours. "When I'm a successful actor, we'll live in California, which you love, and be able to spend more time together," or "I'm spending so much time worrying about the bills that I can't concentrate on my work at the office," or, "You're right. We should both see other people and discover what we really mean to each other."

The strongest weapon in your supporting characters' arsenal is their presence. If all arguments fail, they might decide to end the relationship, either temporarily or permanently. This is another method of trying to control your life. Only you can decide if what the relationship offers is more important than your objectives. Be aware of the fact that this is often a strategy, an attempt to direct your actions to achieve their objective. By surrendering, you give up your freedom to act on your own.

The first thing many people attempt in a situation of competing objectives is to change the other person. By doing that you only lose sight of your own goals. You cannot change another person and it is useless to try. It is a power you do not have. You can enforce behavior, but you cannot change the basic person. This is a lesson some people never learn; they waste their entire lives in an effort to do so.

Your objective should never be to make another person change, but to change the structure of the relationship itself. Changing your actions will do this. For example, a husband has been trying for fifteen years to get his wife's attention. Every morning he demands it. Every morning they fight, and their relationship is a continuing battle. Then one morning he attempts a new action—he makes an emotional appeal, implores, or teases. Suddenly his wife is forced to find a new action to respond to him. She compliments him. Or teases him in return. Their relationship has changed.

A daughter has spent her entire life challenging her mother. There has been tension between them since she was a child, and neither is willing to change, although both are unhappy with the relationship. Suddenly, instead of challenging her mother, she implores, "Help me." Her mother has no ingrained defense against that. All her barriers, the obstacles, have been built on criticism, defiance, and her ability to dominate her daughter. So this new action of the daughter gets through these defenses and the mother is forced to find a new action to respond. The entire structure of the relationship has changed.

This technique of substituting new and unexpected actions is often used by corporations to keep customers from taking actions. You call the telephone company and you're very angry, ready to report the company to the Public Service Commission. "Listen," you scream at an operator, "three months ago you brought me a juice can and a wire and said it was temporary until you got a unit in here. I've been talking into this can for three months and I've had it." Your objective is to get them to install a new telephone immediately. You see it as a crisis situation. Your actions are to demand, to protest, to intimidate.

The phone company has taught its operators conciliatory actions. Instead of offering resistance to your actions, they agree with you. "You're absolutely right. It's an immorality and I don't blame you for being angry. You are perfectly right in your indignation and we'll do something about it as soon as possible."

How do you respond to that?

By offering no resistance or obstacles, the phone company has achieved its objective. In all probability you will not follow through on your threat. They have avoided a crisis situation.

This interplay of competing actions creates conflict. In a play, each character has a particular objective and takes actions to accomplish it. The collision of objectives makes up the drama of the play. It is the most creative character who can select the proper actions to reach his objective. The character who has the greatest reservoir of actions will enjoy a distinct advantage over the others. In life, the person who can draw on the widest range of actions enjoys that advantage.

Not every supporting character in the cast of your play is going to try to prevent you from attempting changes. Some people will be truly supporting, making your efforts easier. Even those people who fight you may well be taking their actions out of great love for you, convinced they are preserving something important.

Consider the objectives of the rest of your cast. Try to understand why they attempt specific actions. If their objectives conflict with yours, find a middle ground, a common sense compromise. When the objectives of two or more people coincide, and the proper actions are chosen, your play has an excellent chance for a long and successful run.

Your ability to make real changes in your life will be greatly determined by your success in dealing with those around you. Every action you take will cause a reaction, and the effectiveness of your action will depend on your ability to recognize and meet this challenge. You must learn when to change your actions or modify your objectives. This is the real game of life.

If you have difficulty competing with your supporting players, you may be forced to make a vital decision: Is the change you are attempting worth threatening important relationships? Only you can answer that question, but it is important to remember that relationships are made stronger when an involved party becomes happier and more satisfied with his life. When people who fear change understand that it may be beneficial, the existing relationship will probably be improved.

It's your show—don't let your supporting characters upstage you.

SCENE: PRODUCED AND DIRECTED BY . . .

You are the bows from which your children are living arrows sent forth.

—KAHLIL GIBRAN

Every theatrical production begins with the producers. They take the original material from the writer, help shape the script, hire production people for jobs ranging from director to gaffer, and cast the actors. They raise money to support the production, negotiate contracts, argue with the unions, and receive a substantial portion of any profits. The people who actually invest in the show are known as backers, or "angels."

But once the creative process begins, once the cast is assembled and the play has to be pounded into shape, the director becomes all-powerful. It is the director who interprets the script, controls the technicians, gives the moment-to-moment orders, and begs, threatens, pleads, or cajoles the best possible performance from his actors. The director can create brave new worlds, as George Lucas did in *Star Wars*, turn winter into summer by pasting leaves onto Georgetown, Washington, trees, as Billy Friedkin did for *The Exorcist*, or even invent history, as Francis Ford Coppola did in creating his *Godfather* saga.

In your life, your parents were both your producers and directors. They created you, and then helped mold you. As a parent, you are also both producer and director. You have complete responsibility for "getting the show on the road." Cast into a role by your parents, who were acting as producers, you do the same thing for your children. As you do, your parents cast your type, provided you with props and role models, and tried to direct you to perform their script to their satisfaction.

This scene is about parents, your own parents, and the parent you may become or perhaps are. Although parents are backers, too often they cannot be called angels.

The majority of parents somehow manage to put together shows that eventually go out on the road and run for a lifetime, but the way they are stuck together often leaves rocky moments in the performance. These bumps are never quite straightened out and the play is never completely satisfying. The play never reaches its full potential.

Parents mean well in their role as producers. No sane person would intentionally harm his or her own children. Most parents do love their children and try to help them become adults capable of getting the most out of life. After spending years watching the mangled results of their efforts, it's important for me to remember that. Parents do mean well. No matter how brutal they can sometimes be, no matter how much punishment they inflict on their children, no matter how deep the scars they've carved, parents do mean well.

During a personalization one of my students remembered it was his father who broke his arm during his almost weekly beating. He later began to understand that he enlisted in the Army and volunteered for Vietnam duty, where he was wounded, to prove to his father that he could "take it like a man."

A woman, one of the leading models in the fashion industry, had no animation in her hands while performing. She completely lost the ability to express herself with her hands when her stepmother punished her by holding them over an open stove burner.

Another man seemed to be laminated in plastic. He was slickly handsome, but nothing about him seemed real. He stopped showing emotion and learned to try to please everyone after being punished for talking back to his mother. His punishment consisted of crawling on his bare knees across a kitchen floor covered with hard dried peas.

One potential actress had five brothers and sisters. Each year her parents would explain to the children that the car was only big enough for four of them, and the remaining two could not go on vacation. Then they would draw lots. Four slips supposedly had "yes" written on them, but her father's favorite joke was to write "no" on all six. He considered it teasing.

I have worked with people who, as children, had been locked in closets for extensive time periods, who had been sexually abused, or had not been loved at all.

These are not punishments. These are certified tortures. It's almost unbelievable that any parent would inflict these horrors on their own children, yet most parents believe they are doing it for the good of the child. It is their method for teaching proper behavior. They really do mean well.

Not all parents behave like this, and not all of my students suffer from the effects of their parents. Some had wonderful childhoods and were encouraged by loving parents, while others remember things being worse than they actually were. But I've seen enough adults suffering from childhood trauma to understand the lasting, devastating effects.

In various ways, people spend their entire lives suffering from their childhood, trying to successfully resolve the problems of the primary parent-child relationship. "Death ends a life," Robert Anderson wrote in his teleplay and movie, *I Never Sang for My Father*, "but it doesn't end a relationship, which struggles on in the survivor's mind toward some resolution which it never finds." In earlier chapters I've discussed the dramatic impact of these relationships, which may be manifested in bad posture, nervous "habits," loss of the free use of the body, complete inability to attempt new actions, loss of identity, or even suicidal tendencies. The ability to initiate real change in life is often blocked by the feelings left over from these relationships. Types and characters become permanently fixed, as people believe they must behave a certain way, because this behavior guaranteed somewhat painless survival. Even if they are not happy or satisfied with their life, they persist in the same pattern because they are no longer in pain.

In order to make the substantial changes necessary to improve the quality of your life, it is necessary to begin by removing all the restraints imposed by your parents. That's where the problems began. You must finally allow yourself to feel the anger you were afraid to show, remembering that it started as love. You innocently expressed your love for your parents and, if it was not accepted or acknowledged and you were made to feel your love was not worthwhile, the emotion didn't just disappear. It became anger, the means to deal with rejection. But few parents allowed their children to express their anger without punishment, so it had to be held in check and helped clog up the expression of all the other emotions.

One point I stress in every exercise, and something you must be aware of, is that it is permissible to get angry at your parents. If you think about it, it is totally inhuman for a parent to spank a child, or worse, without allowing the child to express his feelings about it. It's ridiculous to believe a child should not get angry at his parents just because the punishment is for his own good. This is not to say a child should be allowed to take any actions he wants. Children certainly should not be permitted to slug a parent or break up furniture, but they must be allowed to express their legitimate feelings. These emotions are the most natural thing in the world. It is pretending they don't exist, or shouldn't exist, that creates serious problems.

Don't run to the phone to call your parents and scream at

them, or let loose the torrent of love and hate feelings you've been holding back for so long. The basic exercises you should be doing—personalizations aimed at freeing the body, voice, and emotions—are the means to settle the relationship. These imaginary confrontations will not change your parents at all; they will never even know they happened. But the exercises will help you to change and, by doing that, change the entire relationship as it exists today. I constantly remind my students that it is futile to try to change anyone else's behavior; however, by changing your own actions and intentions you can achieve the same goal—a major change in your relationship.

The father of one of my students used to beat him regularly, until this student learned to defy him by suppressing all feeling. It became a matter of honor for him that his father could not make him cry. In class, after many personalizations about his father, he reached out with an open hand. The moment I reached out and held it, as his father never did, he broke down and began crying. For the first time he allowed himself to feel love for his father and put it into words. "I love you," was all he said.

On his next visit home he took his father into his arms and held him, also for the first time, and he told him that he loved him. Then he wept. He didn't ask for any love in return; he didn't expect to change his father, but he needed to express his own repressed feelings.

His father had no idea how to respond. He was embarrassed. He didn't know how to tell his son that he loved him, but he was profoundly moved. Suddenly he began doing things for his son. He expressed interest in his acting career and his life in New York. He began talking about his own difficult childhood. He never really changed; until he died he remained a taciturn man. His son, by changing himself, by allowing himself to express long-buried emotions, altered the entire relationship.

It was the beginning of major changes in his life.

One of the most curative aspects of my work comes when a student realizes that some parents are incapable of demonstrating love to their children and will always be that way. Worse, and more difficult to deal with, is the possibility that their parents did not love them, for there are many parents who not only don't love their children, but actively express their resentment of them. Once this particular student understood that his father was incapable of expressing love for anyone, not just his children, he began to change.

The material given to you by your parents is probably still shaping your life. You are what they made you. This can prevent you from becoming the total person you are capable of being. Your basic type and character were molded when you were a small child, before you possessed the intellectual capability to deal rationally with them. Now all the intellect in the world, all the "knowing" that that time is over, will not remove the results. These problems must be dealt with emotionally, as they were formed, and that is the purpose of the exercises.

Now is the time to end the emotional domination of your parents. Whatever damage they did should finally be erased. Continue to work with the basic exercises; make personalizations with your parents and authority figures and understand what is happening. You are finally getting free enough to write your own show.

Once you have worked to resolve your own problems with your parents, it's vitally important not to inflict the same damage on your own children. As a parent you have more power and greater responsibility than any director. It is your job to shape the life of a human being, just as your parents tried to do with you. And, as you can see from some of the results I've discussed, this is not an easy job to do well. The decisions you make will influence your children for the rest of their lives. By making the wrong choices you can damage their future; you can plant seeds of unhappiness which will bloom years from now. No one wants this to happen. No one consciously sets out to be a bad parent. But, somehow, sometimes even through the expression of love, it happens. The question is, as director, how can you avoid making these mistakes?

Most important of all, be yourself. The more complete you are as a person, the easier it will be to raise your child. As in every other relationship, the healthier you are, the better the relationship will be. The parents that seem to have the most trouble with their children are those people who do not seem to have access to their own feelings. Instead of just exposing their real emotions to their children, they try to figure out what type of parent to be. They try to act the role of the ideal parent, the "Father Knows Best" role created by Robert Young, without having any idea how to play it. And when something drastic happens, when they are forced to abandon that role, there is nothing to replace it but anger or frustration at having failed.

Much of the damage parents do to their children is caused by their inability to resolve their own childhood problems. If an adult was free of his own hangups, inhibitions, and fears, he would be unlikely to pass them on to his children. Instead, people unable to overcome or deal with these problems, may try to resolve them through their children. They try so hard not to repeat the mistakes their parents made by being too strict or too lenient, by not showing any emotion or smothering their children in emotion, that they bend over too far in the opposite direction. Since they were not perfect, they want their children to be perfect. And, when their kids prove to be only normal, they resort to physical or mental punishment.

It is imperative that the my-parents-treated-me-this-way-so-I'll-never-treat-my-kids-that-way cycle be broken. This can be done by finally resolving your own relationship with your producers. The personalizations can be used to do exactly that.

The best way to deal with a child is to bring all of yourself to him. Children need the experience of real emotions as much as they need knowledge about the practical world. They have to see that their parents are free to express love and anger. People who are inhibited, who cannot express emotions, almost always pass their inhibitions on to their children. If a child is not taught to express his feelings openly, he will find it extremely difficult to do so as he matures. If he finds his feelings are unacknowledged, or rebuffed, he will repress them. It is as simple as that.

Any emotion a child brings to you is good. It makes no difference whether that emotion is love, hate, anger, sorrow, or embarrassment. Good parents not only allow their children the full range of emotions, but support these feelings with love. As I've said, it makes no sense for a parent to have the authority to punish a child, or withhold love, or deprive the child of something, and not expect that child to get angry. The child has to be shown that getting angry doesn't mean that love no longer exists and that anger doesn't have to be expressed through a physical action. Anger is probably the most difficult emotion to deal with, but if the child is allowed to express his anger openly, without fear of unreasonable punishment, he will be much less protective of the other emotions. Anger is the tough one to deal with. The most intelligent thing a parent can tell his child is, "You're angry at me and that's all right, but you still don't get to go to the movies Saturday night because you did something wrong and you're being punished. So go ahead and get as angry as you like."

It is not so much *what* you teach a child as *how* you teach him. The exchange of information is a highly creative moment. Some very successful parents do not have the knowledge of unsuccessful parents, but they convey what they have totally. At that moment they are completely "with" the child. The child is aware of this. Children watch. They feel information coming to them through observation and experience, though they may not understand the words or the concept.

A child takes in information from a parent on all levels. He is aware how that information is being communicated, and that is more important than the facts.

It is not easy to bring yourself completely to every moment of interaction with your child. After working all day, it's difficult to summon up enthusiasm for sharing a homework assignment when what you really want to do is relax and read the newspaper. But these are the important moments, the times when you may reject your child and not even be aware that you're doing so. The child had a need and it was not fulfilled. The next time he will be less likely to look to you for fulfillment.

The two most important things to remember are: Bring yourself completely to every moment of interchange with your child. Allow your child the full range of his emotions.

This entire book, and much of my teaching, would not be necessary if parents had allowed their children expression of the natural emotions. But they did not. Parents help establish barriers, inflict emotional pain, and cause permanent damage, usually in the name of love. I see the results in class all the time. I see students afraid to show love or anger for fear of rejection.

The more complete you become, the more you understand your relationship with your own producers, the better director you will become.

The job of producer-director is never an easy one. Unbelievable complications are always arising. But on opening night, when the show is finally ready to exist without your prodding or shouting, you will stand in the back of the theatre and watch with all the pride of . . . a parent.

It is your baby.

SCENE: THE AUDIENCE

He who lives for applause puts his happiness in the hands of strangers.

—WILL ROGERS

The audience is an always changing, faceless mass. Everything the actor does is aimed at arousing feeling from the audience. The same lines, the same jokes, the same movements affect each audience in a slightly different way, and there is no way of predicting any response. Often the excitement that exists at one performance is replaced by a general feeling of malaise the next. If the audience reacts positively to his performance, the actor is elated; if that same audience does not respond, he may become depressed. The actor needs the audience for his nourishment.

All people play to an unidentifiable audience. They select certain actions or take no actions at all, because they are worried about their appearance in other people's eyes. What other people? Everyone. Them. The audience of our minds. The people we want to like us, to respect us, to love us.

You probably spend time wondering and worrying about what other people think of you. Although you may not know who these other people are, exactly, they limit your actions. You try to take actions that will be socially acceptable, that will not cause "them" to think less of you.

If you're like most people, you are incapable of going up to a stranger and introducing yourself; you probably find it difficult to walk into a room full of strangers; and you're very apprehensive when meeting someone for the first time. You have already convinced yourself that this "audience" will not like your performance—even before you've risked walking to center stage. You've allowed baseless fears and insecurities to dominate your actions.

What you forget is that everyone else is also playing to this unknown audience. While you're wondering what someone else will think of you, positive they are watching every move you make, chances are that person is worrying what you will think of them. People are self-centered. Generally they spend most of their energy developing their own role. They are primarily concerned with reaching their own goals, and have no time to criticize your performance. In their play, at best you are only a supporting character.

Most often there is no audience watching you. You are free to take whatever actions you desire. Only when other people become directly involved in your actions will they turn their attention to your performance. The audience that prevents you from acting is imaginary. It is the universal excuse for being unable to take control of your own life. There is no "them."

Great actors do not play to the audience; they perform the role as they believe it should be done. You too must eliminate the audience from your mind. It is up to you to be the star of your own play.

SCENES: CRITICS

There is no success so small that someone won't find fault with it.

Critics are the bane of every actor. A critic can make or break a show or career with just a few hundred words. Qualified critics are among the most knowledgeable people in the entertainment world, versed in the history, legend, and lore of their particular fields. They are professionals and take their great responsibility seriously. The primary job of the critic is to evaluate a work, and not, as performers sometimes believe, to find fault with everything. A good critic is an expert in his field who can draw on a vast store of experience in reviewing a play or a movie.

Almost everyone plays critic from time to time. Everyone has opinions, makes judgments, and finds ways to express them. Actually, being this type of critic is easy. All you have to do is find something you don't like, don't appreciate, or don't understand, and comment upon it. No knowledge or expertise is necessary. This type of critic is not to be confused with the professional, of course.

We all become the subject of criticism. I have heard it said that there is no success so small that someone won't find fault with it. Our parents are our first critics. Their criticism helps shape our performance because we don't have the option of not heeding their advice. These critics hold the purse strings; they have all the power. As we grow older and receive criticism from teachers, friends, even loved ones, we begin to have the choice of whether or not to consider its merits.

Criticism should not be quickly dismissed. It can be extremely valuable. Other people can see things in you that you might not be aware of, and their suggestions, their criticism can be extremely valuable. It can also be detrimental. Criticism offered for the wrong reasons or by the wrong person can cause permanent emotional damage. From what I have seen, a great amount of criticism is tendered for the wrong reasons.

I attended the opening night party celebrating one of the biggest smash musicals in recent years. The star of the show was being showered with unanimous praise from every professional critic. That night, after many years of hard work, she became a star. Yet, during this party her mother leaned over and confided in a soft, almost shaming voice, just loudly enough so a very few people could hear, "I saw you miss your point on that turn in the second act." She said nothing else. She offered no compliments. This was perhaps the most important moment in her daughter's life and she felt it was necessary to bring up this totally insignificant criticism. Her only possible reason for doing this was to establish her own importance. The star was shaken by this, upset far beyond the significance of these few small words, just as her mother knew she would be.

Offering criticism allows people to become more important than they would otherwise be. It enables them to feel superior and helps them deal with their feelings of jealousy.

People can be very jealous of success. This is something often seen in the entertainment world. Stage mothers who push their child to every audition suddenly become terribly jealous when the child becomes successful. They see the child attaining a position or accomplishing something they were never able to do. This happens outside the theatre, too. Anyone who has attempted to diet knows how difficult it is to stay on a diet when unsuccessful dieters are around. Your success reminds them of their failure, and they will do everything possible to destroy your diet.

If you get a raise, meet the person of your dreams, manage to buy something special, receive attention, get your name in the paper, get invited to a nice party, or even manage to jog three miles, someone is going to be envious. Often they will express their envy through criticism, "That's a nice car you bought. I guess you know about all the overheating problems they have," or "A man your age should be more careful about exercising. You might have a heart attack."

Critics often speak to you from their own disappointments. The primary movie critic of a major weekly newsmagazine has been diligently writing movie scripts in his free time. Some theatre critics are failed playwrights, book reviewers unsuccessful authors, and food critics lousy cooks. That does not necessarily mean they are bad critics.

The most important thing for you to do when subject to criticism is to consider the source. Don't accept all criticism as justified, nor dismiss it as jealousy. By understanding the objectives of the person who offers the criticism, you can decide if the criticism is justified. If you are dating someone a friend or acquaintance is attracted to, it would be wise to be wary of her criticism. If, on the other hand, a close friend who has nothing to gain offers criticism, it is probably worth paying attention.

Criticism can often be positive. Learning which critics in your life offer constructive aid can be very beneficial. We all need someone we trust to offer advice, and that should be the primary function of your critic.

There are numerous methods to deal with rude or uncalled for criticism. Actress Sylvia Miles dumped a plate of linguini over the head of magazine critic John Simon. Producer David Merrick found working people with the same names as influential New York City newspaper critics and printed their favorable reviews of his Broadway Show, *Subways Are for Sleeping*. It should be easier for you to deal with criticism.

Know where it is coming from. Good criticism includes suggestions for improvement, not just negative comment. If there is no intention to help you, and it does not come from someone who has your interests in mind, ignore it. Pay no attention to it. Critics gain their power because people listen to them. When their advice is scorned, they quickly lose that power.

Some people find it impossible to ignore any kind of criticism. They are so insecure, so ready to admit their own shortcomings, that they not only agree with other people's criticism, they even add some of their own. Diane Keaton would often do that in the workshop. Before I could begin critiquing a scene she performed, she would interrupt and explain, "I know, I know, I was terrible. I just couldn't get into the scene . . ." when, in fact, she was usually excellent.

You may have personal critics, people whose comments you accept without consideration. These may be your parents, who have been making comments for so long you have learned to accept them. The Broadway star could not rebuff any criticism her mother made, no matter how trivial, because she had spent much of her life listening to her mother's advice. Take a moment and consider your personal critics. Just be aware that they exist.

What that musical actress should have done that opening night was turn to her mother and say, "How dare you watch my entire show and have only that to say. I've been dancing for fifteen years, I've been critically acclaimed, and you bring up something like that! You couldn't love me and do that." Of course, her entire upbringing prevented her from taking that action. But during an exercise in class the following week, she did exactly that. She made an improvisation and released all her anger at her mother without provoking a fight. This is exactly what you should try. There are certain critics you will not be able to answer, a parent, an employer, a thoughtless friend. The basic personalization can be utilized to release all your pent-up anger.

Too often we allow criticism to affect us severely. Instead of learning from it, or ignoring it, we react by going into a temporary state of depression. Change, or any attempt to take new actions, becomes impossible. Once again, a member of your supporting cast achieves his or her objective by upstaging the star of your show.

Don't be afraid of criticism. It is impossible to please all critics all the time. And don't react to it without serious consideration. Remember, even *Tobacco Road* opened to mixed reviews.

SCENE: BAD NOTICES

Take each man's censure, but reserve thine own.
—SHAKESPEARE

Dorothy Parker once reviewed the performance of a young actress by noting, "Her emotions ran the gamut from A to B." Luckily, Katherine Hepburn did not allow that blast to destroy her confidence, and became one of our great performers. Bad notices are the occupational hazard of show business. Eventually, every performer is going to be poorly reviewed, and how he reacts to those notices will have an important effect on his career. Some actors try to fight their critics; others use criticism as an impetus to work harder to improve their technique. But everybody gets depressed.

How you react to setbacks in your life will help determine how successful you will be. Some people quit when everything seems to go wrong; others use their failures as the basis of even greater success. But, from time to time, everybody gets depressed.

Depression can be a terrible thing. It can be caused by almost anything. Suddenly you feel lousy, listless; everything seems wrong; your life seems worthless; no one likes you; you feel you are a failure at life. This feeling can be totally debilitating. It can prevent you from functioning normally in the world and is as serious as most physical diseases. The worst aspect of depression is the overriding feeling of being trapped, that there is no way out, things will never improve. Of course, this is not true, but it is almost impossible to understand that when you are in a state of depression.

Actors are forced to learn to live with depression. Even when they feel emotionally awful, they still must go out on stage and do a performance or go to an audition. The actor's life may be a shambles, a close friend or relative may have died, an intense relationship may have ended, but the show absolutely must go on. The actor must go on stage and make a character come to life; he must eliminate his personal problems from his portrayal. If he is performing a comedy, he has to play for laughs, although inside he might be tormented. The technique the actor uses in this situation is the same technique that will work for you. It will allow you to fight your depression and eventually to overcome it.

The actor eliminates depression on stage by throwing himself completely into his part. He becomes his character, leaving his personal problems behind while be basks in the spotlight. It is only afterward, when the curtain is down and he removes his costume, that he can again allow his thoughts to dwell on his depression. While his mind was occupied with lines to remember, stage directions, and audience response, he was able to avoid all negative thoughts, but when it was left free to wander, it settled comfortably into the muck of depression. The key to fighting depression successfully is focusing on positive thoughts and actions.

If that were simple to do, no one would ever feel depressed. It isn't. It takes work. There was a point in my life in which I was mired in a deep depression. Absolutely everything seemed to be going wrong. I was having personal difficulties; I was in debt; and my career was stagnant. My problems didn't seem solvable. I was in emotional pain; I was anxious; I was feeling a failure. There was nothing and no one for me to hold on to to pull myself up out of these depths. I knew I had to start somewhere, but I just couldn't figure out how or where. I had my body and my health. That didn't make me feel any better, but it was a start. I had my thinking powers, but I couldn't control my thoughts. They were all negative. Even as I was thinking about fighting this depression, my mind kept telling me that it was hopeless.

I had to find some positive thoughts to erase my negative feelings. I reminded myself that I had never felt this way in my entire life. I remembered days when I felt good. I remembered when I felt anything was possible. What was it, I wondered, that was missing in my life? What did I have then that I had lost?

I decided to create a series of positive images. That would be a start. I looked through magazines to find pictures to which I responded positively. A picture of a dog. A pretty lakeside scene. People I admired. I cut out anything that made me feel better and pasted it into a notebook. Under each picture I wrote three sentences explaining the positive things I felt from each one. Beneath a picture of a boy fishing in a lake I wrote, "I want tranquility. I want security. I want peace of mind." After a brief period, I had filled ten pages with pictures. At night I would sit in a comfortable chair and just stare at each one. I would try to etch it into my memory. I would try to *feel* the positive thoughts that it communicated.

What I was doing, although I didn't realize it then, was learning how to control my attention. At first it was very difficult. I would think of these pictures and briefly feel better, but then negative thoughts would intrude. But as long as I could focus my attention on these positive images and thoughts, the negative thoughts were absent. Eventually I had twenty-five pictures and was able to concentrate for about twenty minutes, uninterrupted by negation.

When I finally felt strong enough to try to audition, I got on the subway to begin making my round of calls on agents and casting directors. A flow of negative thoughts raced into my mind. I didn't try to resist them. Instead, I closed my eyes and imagined my pictures. For the first time, I started getting free of the depression. For twenty minutes I concentrated attention on positive things. For twenty minutes no negative thoughts intruded.

I was using my mind and emotion, but not my body. So I

began going to a nearby park and jogging. As I ran, I tried to recall the positive images and the thoughts I had written about them. Each day I ran just a little farther than the previous day and was free of destructive thoughts for a short while longer.

Logically, I knew I couldn't spend all day concentrating on having positive thoughts. I had to take this control and utilize it outside my body. So, instead of remembering images, I began bringing my attention to the environment. As will be explained in Chapter Nine, I looked for colors. I tried to find everything green, for example. Trees, leaves, somebody's sneakers. Then I moved my attention to another color, and then sounds and objects. Eventually I managed to stretch these periods of concentrating to over an hour. That enabled me to function and to feel better. Eventually time and constructive effort healed most of the original causes of my depression.

I still have my notebook, and gaze through it from time to time. But I have since spent years developing the exercise system contained in this book, and that work has enabled me to control my thoughts. I still occasionally get depressed, as everyone does, but my depression no longer controls me. I simply don't allow my mind to dwell on negative thoughts.

The best way for you to fight depression is to prepare for it, to begin taking preventive measures now. The more you practice the exercises you've learned, the more control you will have over your mind and body. You may not be able to eliminate depression, but you will be able to prevent it from becoming debilitating. By being able to focus your mind, you will have a weapon against the seemingly hopeless influx of negative thoughts. One of my female students fought her depression by jogging every day. She had never liked running and hated the thought of making circles around a track. But running every day enabled her to feel that she had some control over her life, that she could make some decisions.

The exercises you have learned will enable you to bring some order to the disorder of depression.

Dealing with depression does not always solve the problems that caused it. The sooner you can remedy these problems, the sooner your depression will disappear. But the longer you are able to free your thoughts from negative feelings, the easier it will be to take positive actions along these lines.

Depression does have real causes. It is not an irrational state of mind you suddenly created. Often the causes are obvious, death, destruction, a mistake, failure, boredom, and lack of fulfillment are only a few. But on occasion the causes are not so obvious. You sort of slide into a feeling of being trapped, of not really having control of your own life, of having missed all the opportunities that once seemed available to you. In order to fight depression, it is first necessary to isolate the cause. Figure out what it is that is making you feel bad. Then try to understand what you'll have to do to solve these problems. In some instances, the death of a friend, for example, there will be little you can do. Time will pass and eventually you will feel better. You can fill your mind with positive thoughts and lovely memories as often as possible, but there is nothing you can do to rectify the cause. Only time will heal. However, if the causes of your depression are things you have allowed to happen, you can take steps to effect change. The purpose of this book is to help you to change your life. Consider it an instruction manual and use it to deal with those things that have caused you to become depressed. Once these problems are solved, your depression will disappear.

Depression can't always be prevented, but it can be limited. When you are in a depressed state, return to the exercises. They will enable you to at least focus your attention and energy and to temporarily eliminate negative thoughts. Using personalizations, you may also be able to deal with some of the more deeply hidden problems that have caused this state to occur.

The most important thing you can do while depressed is to keep busy. It doesn't even matter what you do, as long as you continue doing it. The busier you are, the more occupied your mind will be. It is during your slack periods, when you're not working, when you have nothing scheduled, that these exercises will be of the most value. Do not allow your depression to overwhelm your normal life. You must go to work. You must continue to make plans. You must spend time with your friends. No matter how difficult this all might seem, particularly while you are depressed, it is the best way to deal with this state.

How do you feel right now? If you answered, "Good," or "Okay," you've already started preparing for your next bout with depression. Often when people are depressed, they can't remember or feel anything else but the state they are in. It feels as if they have been depressed all their life and they can't see anything but a life of depression ahead of them. By sensorily recording the various emotional highs of well-being, joy, and satisfaction on your memory, you will be able to recall them during your depression. The recollection that there are other, better states of being will help you to break the grip of depression. These memories are the tools that will help you dig your way out of that seemingly bottomless pit.

SCENE: COSTUMES

For the apparel oft proclaims the man.

—SHAKESPEARE

Clothes do not make the man. Or, for that matter, the woman. What they really do is reveal or conceal the individual. They are accessories, and if they are properly used, they can help you present a complete statement of your type and character. They help you make a statement about yourself. The man who first said clothes make the man was probably the man who made the clothes.

Costuming is a vitally important part of theatre. The object of the costume designer is to arrange each character's clothing so the audience will immediately recognize his type. A man wearing a tailored suit is meant to be taken more seriously than a man in faded blue jeans and work shirt. When a female character appears in a fur coat, the audience understands that she is part of the establishment, she is not poor, and is reasonably sophisticated. From the earliest movie days, the good guys wore white and the bad guys black.

Clothes always make a statement about the person who is wearing them. On occasion, they become a focal point. Pianist Liberace built an entire career around his outrageous clothing and props. In the play *Coco*, the story of designer Coco Chanel, the magnificent gowns were vital to the success of the show. Richard Burton performed *Hamlet* in modern dress on the Broadway stage, adding an exciting element to the play. And in *Hair*, the lack of costumes made the strongest statement.

You put on a costume every day. Some people put on two, a work costume and a leisure-time costume. Your choice of clothing is an expression to the world that you feel a certain way about yourself. Clothes are an external manifestation of your internal person. Some people, for example, use clothing as camouflage. Instead of dressing to be seen, they dress to hide themselves from the world. One actress used to wear only baggy pants, bulky sweaters, and a jacket to hide the attractive body she had somehow come to believe was ugly. Dark clothes which will hopefully blend in with the background are favored by people who don't want to be noticed. Others use clothing to draw attention to themselves or to make a social statement. They make a point of wearing blatantly offbeat clothing as a way of saying, "Look at me. I am an individual and I refuse to conform to outdated social codes." There is nothing wrong with this. But when you do it, you should be aware that other people recognize your intention.

Society tends to identify a person by his costume. A policemen is helpful. An athlete has certain talents. An ice cream man is friendly. A girl in a small bikini is sexy. Your everyday costume also signals something to the rest of the world. It reveals you as a certain type of person. It expresses your standards, and your lifestyle. People similar to you will respond to this signal; people very different will stay away. Clothes help establish a common ground. They let you know the people with whom you might be compatible. In the business world a woman who wears pantsuits is considered less feminine and more serious than one who accents her sexuality. Many major corporations understand the psychological significance of clothes and set up dress codes for their employees. General Motors, for example, once expected its top executives to wear conservative white shirts. When a young newcomer to management wore a pale yellow shirt instead, he was branded a radical.

You should be fully aware of the fact that your costume makes an impression on other people and take advantage of it. If you want to fit in, try to reflect the clothing worn by the people around you. If you want to stand out, deviate from the accepted codes. Decide what are your best physical features and wear clothes to accent them. Obviously you don't want to overdo it, and good taste should always be considered. You should also wear clothes that hide your least appealing points.

Because clothes are so important in making an impression on other people, I often draw the attention of my students to their dress. Sometimes I demand that certain students change the way they dress for class. I insist they wear a type of clothing opposite from what they normally wear. My belief is that if you break the external behavior, you allow the internal person new ways of coming into the world again. One young woman constantly wore dark pants and tops to class. I asked her to wear light-colored dresses or skirts and tops. Her whole personality changed when she wore different clothes. She became light and cheerful, like her costume.

Knowing your costume makes a statement should remind you to consider your dress when preparing to take actions. Your clothes can either support your actions or confuse them. It makes no sense to wear a tie and jacket if your intention is to be casual. It makes no sense for a woman to wear lace or frilly clothing if she intends to be commanding. If you dress in opposition to your intentions, wearing old jeans to an important meeting, for example, all you will do is confuse the people you are dealing with. Their attention will be drawn to your clothing. Rather than supporting your actions, your clothing will detract from them.

Props can also be extremely beneficial. A prop can be anything that you use to your advantage. Understanding the correct use of props can help you to achieve your objective. Actors, of course, must learn how to handle props early in their careers. Great scene stealers understand how to use props to draw the attention of the audience. Tallulah Bankhead was perhaps the greatest.

A presumptuous young actress in the same show with Tallulah warned her that she was going to make the audience forget the great star. "My deah," Tallulah explained, "I can hold the attention of the audience without even being on stage." That night she proceeded to do exactly that. Just before her exit, she was supposed to place a coffee cup on a table. Instead of doing that, she placed it on the very edge of the table. The cup balanced precariously, and the audience watched intently to see if it would fall while the young actress stood across the stage reciting her climactic lines.

You can use numerous props to your own advantage. George Hamilton created a sensation when he arrived in

California in a Rolls Royce. He had no acting credits, but he did have that car, and attracted attention. As an experiment, I tried carrying a simple walking stick. The result was that I was suddenly treated very differently than before. People stepped out of the way for me in the subway. That stick set me apart from the rest of the crowd. People did not know exactly how to deal with me, so they moved out of my way. Any new or different item you carry or wear will create a whole different set of responses to you. Try wearing a hat or ascot, or change the length of your hair, and you will see how easy it is to draw attention to yourself.

As an exercise, select one piece of clothing that you would not normally wear, or find a prop you would not normally use. For some people this may be a tie, for others it may be a belt buckle or a hat. Observe the way people observe you. By doing something out of the ordinary, you will change the way other people perceive you. This can be used to your advantage. Don't overdo it. Just utilize a new piece of clothing or prop and bring your attention to the effect it creates.

Take your appearance into consideration when planning your actions. It does make a difference. Even the cast of *Hair* understood this naked truth.

CHAPTER NINE:
The Set—Making a Scene

Authority and place demonstrate and try the tempers of men, by moving every passion and discovering every frailty.

—PLUTARCH

The curtain rises. Before us is the setting—a few pieces of canvas, a little paint, wood, fabric, some props, lighting, and a lot of imagination. With these tools the scenic designer can transport the audience from a dirt farm on "Tobacco Road," beyond the galaxies to "Via Galactica." A set is an illusion, a suggestion that an entire world exists beyond the single spot portrayed. It is the foundation upon which the magic of dramatic creation unfolds.

The primary purpose of the set is to aid in the creation of plot and characters, to help establish a mood. According to the great theatrical designer Robert Edmond Jones: "The designer creates an environment in which all noble emotions are possible. Then he retires. The actor enters. If the designer's work has been good, it disappears from our consciousness at that moment. We do not notice it anymore."

Everything that you do also takes place on a set. It can be a single dirty room on New York City's Bowery, or Disneyland's Magic Castle, but it is still a set. Unlike actors, we fail to take full advantage of our surroundings—our "place"—to help us get what we want. Instead, like the audience, we admire it, then forget it.

Understanding how to use a "place" to your own advantage can be crucial to the successful completion of whatever actions you choose. The right setting can help complete the action, the wrong setting can make it more difficult, or even impossible. Occasionally the set itself becomes the focus of attention and causes, forces, or changes your intended action. Therefore, it is to your benefit to observe, analyze, and, when possible, manipulate the setting to help you make precisely the points you intend to make.

During the filming of a big-budget movie in New York City, one of Hollywood's leading men was obnoxiously pursued by a would-be starlet. It was obvious to everyone, including this actor, that she intended to use him to land a part in the movie. The more he resisted, the more aggressive she became. Finally, he decided to settle matters. He began by inviting her to his hotel suite for dinner.

A few hours before her scheduled arrival, I walked by his room. The place was a mess. Porters were carrying out what seemed to be all the furniture and decorations. Mirrors and paintings were carted out with sofas and tables. The actor was busy supervising them.

He was elegantly dressed by the time the young women arrived. He opened the door and invited her in. She took two steps into the room and stopped. There, sitting in the middle of the otherwise bare living room, was a big double bed. Without a word, the woman turned and walked out.

This is known as using the setting to make a point.

Rarely is the meaning of an environment so easily understood, but every "place" is designed for a purpose. It may be decorated to calm, to dominate, to charm, or to impress, and it may have been done subconsciously, but it was put together with an objective in mind. Understanding that objective, then choosing intentions that work with, rather than against it, can help you achieve exactly what you want. If, for example, you walk into an executive's lavish office and find an expensive desk on a raised platform and original art covering the wall, you can be sure the room was decorated to give the impression that the executive is a busy, important, sophisticated, tasteful man. The room lends itself to actions of domination, commanding, and impressing. Knowing this, it would be a mistake for you to attempt actions to dominate, command, or impress him. Those are *his* intentions. Yours might be to admire the office, or placate; you'd probably be able to establish a rapport by using either of them. On the other hand, if the office is stark and the only things hanging on the wall are a picture of the company president, a chart of the executive leadership, and a collection of degrees and licenses, it should be obvious to you that this is the office of a very businesslike person. Your actions should stress your competence and professionalism, and they should be right to the point, matching the environment this person has established.

You should utilize your own environment precisely the same way. I try to do it with my small office. There are three chairs, one swivel-back, one comfortable, and one hard-back desk chair, a roll-top desk, a glass-door bookcase, a curtained window, and an Oriental rug. I rearrange the furniture depending on who is expected. If a working director is coming by, for example, I'm certainly not going to try to overwhelm him with my importance. My intention is to make him comfortable. I'll set up two chairs facing each other in front of the window, and offer him the more comfortable chair.

If, on the other hand, someone is coming to discuss a subject I'm not particularly interested in, I'll sit at my cluttered desk. My intention here will be to convey the fact that I'm very busy, that I haven't much time. Usually the meeting will be quickly concluded.

Almost everyone, sometimes without realizing it, has created a "place" to aid their intention. You clean your home when company is expected, your object being to impress your visitors. The most important thing to remember when setting up a place is your objective. What is the purpose of the room? What do you want to accomplish in this room? Is it for your own relaxation, or do you intend to use it to impress business associates? Do you want to encourage conversation or discourage it? Once you know your objective, everything in the room should be there only to aid you in accomplishing it. If it is a workroom, then it should be specifically suited for work. Possible distractions, such as a television set, should be removed; it should be well lit; it should have space for your work supplies within easy reach of your work area. If you don't want to be interrupted, chairs for visitors should be uncomfortable and placed far from a table, alone in the middle of the room.

But if the purpose of the room is to charm visitors, then it might include soft lighting that is particularly flattering to you, extremely comfortable furniture placed close together for conversation, a good stereo system, tables within easy reach of the chairs, and all the "props" which will enable you to put someone at complete ease.

These places should be planned with your own particular character in mind, or at least the image you want to project. If you think of yourself as youthful and bursting with exuberance, then you will want the room to be splashed with color. You might hang bright modern art posters on the walls, use modern spot lighting, a lot of glass and brass, and prominently display your stereo system and records. If, on the other hand, you want to present a mature, more subdued image, you might panel at least one wall with wood, include a good deal of book shelving, use comfortable, sturdy traditional furniture, and earth colors throughout the room. To set it all off you might include one modern print, which will show an appreciation of "modern," but a choice of "tradition."

Every place, a restaurant, an office, a living room, even a bathroom, can be used to further your intentions, if you plan them that way. There is no insincerity involved. You travel to a place, or invite people to your place, with a purpose in mind. Whether it is a simple friendly get-together, or a meeting to negotiate a multimillion dollar deal, you choose that specific place for a reason. This is simply a matter of planning and organizing your life to be as effective as possible, something few people do. If you take the time to make these specific choices, you will have an advantage over the majority who don't.

Although most often the place serves as a background, under some circumstances it can become the center of attention. For the people trapped above the raging fire in *The Towering Inferno*, for the passengers on Dean Martin's plane in *Airport*, for the survivors of the capsized ocean liner in *The Poseidon Adventure*, and for the citizens of Los Angeles who suffered through *Earthquake*, the place suddenly and unexpectedly became dominant. Every action was taken in response to a change in the setting. Until that skyscraper caught fire, that plane ran into trouble, that boat flipped over, and that city started shaking, the place served only as a background. Similarly, until you are lost on a lonely road at night, or are alone in a house or apartment and hear strange noises, or have to meet somebody at a specific point, or go somewhere unusual, you are probably not aware of the importance place can have in your life. Most people pay little attention to the effect a place has on their life until their relationship with that place changes.

You are probably not even aware of your surroundings.

Quickly, think: What color is your toothbrush? What is the color or design of the sheets you slept on last night? Describe the floor or rug in the entranceway of the place you work. How many floors are there in your office building? Describe your best friend's sugar bowl. Without looking at your feet—what color are the shoes you're wearing? Finally, why can't you remember all of these common things?

As with most people, you've gotten so used to doing the same tasks, in the same way, in the same place, you've fallen into a behavior pattern. Your daily routine is full of small habits, repeated endlessly without even the recognition that they are habits. They spread from morning to night and have become your lifestyle. Do you get out of bed in the same way every morning, slip into the same slippers left overnight in the same place, prepare for work or your day in the same way, take the same route, the same transportation and see the same people, finally to perform the same labors in about the same way? Nothing changes. You become depressed and unhappy. And you wonder why life has become such a routine.

These small habits, this so-called "lifestyle," can be broken by changing your relationships to the familiar places. As we've seen in every disaster movie, when common relationships to places change, people also change. The weak suddenly become strong, the cowards turn brave, and the coldest reveal tender, warm hearts. By changing your relationship to your "places," you can replace habits with new actions. But in order to change your patterns of behavior, as I said much earlier, it is first necessary to become totally aware of them.

A place, any place, consists of numerous sensory aspects. We describe a place by its most common properties: form, color, temperature, sound, and odor. The same room might be accurately described by the phrases, "bright red," "really cold," "neochaotic furniture," or numerous others. All of the sensory aspects of a "place" are flexible and can be altered. By altering any of them, you change the place. A room can be completely changed with a paint job, or the addition of a rug, or the subtraction of a poster, or by rearranging the furniture. The difference is often amazing.

My purpose is to bring your awareness to the importance of your relationship to a given "place." This recognition of the environment as an aid to fulfilling your actions should be the beginning of a change of place.

COLOR EXERCISE

This exercise will increase your awareness of your surroundings. Start by selecting a color. It makes no difference what color. As you sit in a room, or walk outdoors, or ride, concentrate on finding everything around you in that particular color. Bring the same attention to that color you earlier brought to your breath. You will be absolutely astounded at how colorful the world around you really is, and surprised that you've never been quite aware of it before. Objects of the color you've chosen will seemingly jump out at you. Your toothbrush. Clothes in your closet. Street signs. Window decorations. Book jackets. Automobiles. Buildings. Window shutters. Displays. Things you've passed countless times and never noticed will suddenly grab your full attention.

The following day, select a second color and do precisely the same thing. You'll be stunned at how many perfectly visible objects you failed to see the day before. It isn't necessary to spend more than ten minutes bringing awareness to any particular color, and don't try to do every color in one day. This is a sensory exercise and its object is to reopen you to the world around you, to make you aware of how much goes on around you that you not only don't see, but are not even aware of. This is a method to reconnect you to your environment. It takes time. Like building your body, it is a progressive exercise.

With each new day, select a third color, a fourth, a fifth, and so on.

OBJECT EXERCISE

After you have explored colors to your satisfaction, start bringing your attention to specific objects. For a short period notice nothing but shoes. Look at all the different shapes, colors, and materials. Do the same with hats. It may come as a surprise to you to see how many people, both men and women, are wearing hats again. It happened while you were not paying attention. Look for Volkswagens. Front doors. Nameplates. The objects you pick are not important. This new-found awareness of the multicolored object-filled world around you is important—it's a world full of sensory delights usually taken for granted. It's a feast for your eyes.

One day look for thin people. The next day concentrate on fat people. Just be aware that your world is alive.

Look at tall people one day, and people smaller than you the next.

Eventually, begin to reawaken your other senses in exactly the same way. Start one morning and concentrate on smells. Be aware of the odors you've become so used to you don't even notice them anymore.

SOUNDS

Listen one day just for sounds, sounds so common you no longer hear them. The world is an absolute symphony of sounds: clanging, honking, popping, screeching, chirping, hissing, thumping, thudding, booming sounds. It is the sound of life going on around you, and most people have learned to shut it out.

SENSE COMBINATIONS

After you get used to bringing your concentration to one color or object, sound or smell, try combining two, or even three, different sensory objects. The world, you will discover, is filled with red Volkswagens. There is a great mass of fat people wearing hats, and thin people seem to prefer brown shoes. Eventually, without any effort, and with enjoyment, you'll start seeing the world in composition. You'll begin to reawaken to your environment. As you did as a child, you'll discover that the world around is an exciting, alive place—somehow you've managed to become numb to the myriad sensations it offers.

This most enjoyable exercise should stimulate your awareness of the world around you and its component parts. Now, it's up to you to put these parts together to form your environment. Every room has a basic function. The purpose of a kitchen is to prepare food; a bedroom is to sleep in; a bathroom is to take care of the bodily functions; a den is aimed at relaxation; and a workroom should make it easier for you to work. But each room should make a statement about you that goes beyond that. A kitchen with a carefully selected spot for the most exotic utensils would indicated that the person who used it really understood food, was perhaps a gourmet. A bathroom with a huge tub for lolling would show that the person who selected it was somewhat sensuous. The bedroom, of course, can make many statements. The person whose bedroom is decorated with mirrors on the ceiling, soft lights, a stereo system within easy reach of the headboard, and a waterbed would make a quite different statement and aid in different actions than a bedroom with a traditional bed with a frilly cover over it, no carpets on the floor, a clock radio to provide sound, and a telephone near the top of the bed. Neither one is right or wrong, but they would certainly appeal to different types.

ENVIRONMENT EXERCISE

Make a map of your home and/or office. In each room write the specific purpose the room is intended to be used for. It might be work, entertainment, relaxation, studying, sleeping, or cleanliness. Then, roughly, draw in only the furniture that aids that specific purpose.

These are the essentials. These are the items you must have. At some point, you selected each piece. These items say something about your type and character.

Now draw in the other items in each room. These are the pieces you chose to put in each particular room. They might have been placed anywhere, or not purchased at all. But you selected them because you believed they would add to the environment you were trying to create. Now is the time to decide if you've successfully created that environment. If you have, then taking actions consistent with the environment should be relatively easy, as long as you remain aware that the room is decorated with a purpose in mind.

Now try rearranging the furniture in each room to aid your objective. Some hints: Chairs and sofas placed close together encourage conversation. The television set might be placed in any room. Chairs facing the set instead of each other will limit socializing. Bright lights encourage loud conversation. Wood is considered sophisticated. Rooms can have more than one function, but if a room does, it should be broken down into easily identifiable areas. Try not to locate chairs in regular walk areas. Mirrors make any room look much larger. Anything that is not meant to be touched should be placed on high shelves. Ashtrays indicate that you don't mind people smoking; a lack of ashtrays may mean you discourage it. Never put a bed or seating arrangement in front of a draft window or an air conditioner.

When you are finished, examine each room. What is its function? Does it fulfill that function? What are your usual objectives in the room? Will it aid you in fulfilling these objectives? What does each room say about you as a type and character? Does each room convey the image you are really trying to project? Is that image the real you, or the front you've created over a long period of time?

The last question is a particularly important one. Most people set up environments to allow them to continue already established behavior patterns. They present an image to the world, and use their environment to back it up. So, instead of providing support, or energy, to become the person you are capable of being, the "place" does nothing more than reinforce the behavior that is causing all your problems. For that reason your environment is an importnat place to begin making real changes. Throughout this book we've discussed making changes in your life, changes involving your entire lifestyle. The idea of really changing may seem overwhelming to you. You may be at a loss as to where to begin.

Begin at the beginning. Make small changes first. Since your environment both reflects and supports your current lifestyle, it is best to start by changing your relationship to that environment. That simply involves doing the same old things in brand-new ways. Consciously change the way you perform the most basic actions in your usual "places."

HABIT BREAKING

Try to get out of bed a different way each morning. This should be fun. It should also serve as a reminder that you are consciously making changes in your life. One morning roll off and onto the floor. Try crawling under the sheets and out the base of the bed. Stand up on the bed and walk off. While breaking my own long-established behavior patterns, I started each day this way for almost a year and managed to invent some of the silliest methods of getting out of bed possible. You really haven't tried everything until you've backed off the base of your bed on your hands and knees.

Instead of putting on your shirt or blouse right arm first, start with your left arm. Or vice versa.

Rearrange your usual routine of preparing for work, or the day.

Change your morning beverage. Use a different cup or glass to hold it. Pick it up with the hand other than the one you normally use.

If possible, take a different route to work. Try to continue making these small adjustments at work. If you find it difficult to remember you're making changes, carry a small notepad and write down each change. Eventually just make a notation of your new changes. Comparing the amount of changes from one day to the next will serve as a memory stimulant.

As you begin breaking these minor ingrained habits—at the same time continuing to work on the sensory exercises—you will begin to see how limiting and rigid your normal behavior is. You may even come to believe, as I did, that your life was just one large collection of habits. Breaking habits will help you to discover what else is possible. These little steps should prove to you, as they did to me, that change is possible. Making small changes successfully will also make you feel good about yourself. You should begin seeing changes in your life almost immediately. Certainly your relationship to your "place" and the world around you will change.

Breaking ingrained habits will force you to become aware of how much impact "places" have upon you. This is something it takes many of my students a long time to realize. It is always a positive sign to me when one of my students mentions that that they are moving, or redecorating, or adding some furniture or decorations. This means that they are changing; they are no longer satisfied with their old environment. This is as it should be, because they are no longer the same person who created that old environment.

On occasion I ask a student questions about his "place," because it helps me to learn something about him or her. This information may provide a lead as to which areas to explore to find this student's particular difficulty. I have also found that by suggesting that a student make changes in his "place," even before he begins really changing, I can accelerate changes in his lifestyle.

I remember one student in particular. He might have had some talent, but it was impossible to tell. His whole body attitude was despair, hopelessness, futility. He carried himself like an elderly man and wore baggy and wrinkled clothes. His long hair hung loosely over his eyes, almost completely hiding his face. "I always seem to be so depressed," he told me one afternoon. "I'm always so tired."

I couldn't seem to generate any spark of energy, even anger, in him. "I don't usually ask my students personal questions," I finally explained, "but I don't know where to start with you. Tell me a little about yourself."

Eventually the discussion settled on his apartment. A look of sheer disgust came over him. "It's not too good. It's got these dull brown walls and faded olive drapes. I got a few fruit crates I use for tables and some beat-up old furniture from the Salvation Army. And I have a new, nice dark rug on the floor."

I asked him how many windows his apartment had.

He shrugged. "Two. But since they look right out onto the street, somebody painted them over a long time ago. There's a few cracks in the paint, though, and a little light comes in."

I asked him how this apartment was lighted.

"You know, just the usual bulb hanging from the ceiling." The class was laughing at this whole conversation, of course. It was absurd.

I asked him what kind of music he listened to.

I was not disappointed in his answer. "I like hard rock. I got all the Grateful Dead albums."

It was obvious to everyone in the room why he was always depressed and tired. He was living in a crypt. His "place" was reinforcing his feelings of loneliness, depression, unhappiness. He woke up every day to a bare light bulb and dark walls. What other type mood could he start the day with?

"I've got to get you out in the sun," I told him. "Out in the light where real life takes place." I started him on a minor decorating program, telling him where he could buy cheap drapes and covers for his aging furniture. I told him to immediately go out and buy a paint scraper. I sent him to a store on the lower East Side of New York that carried new clothes at low prices. And I suggested he try some other types of music.

He changed within a few weeks. His entire life did not suddenly bloom, and his face was not always radiant, but he did change. He'd painted the apartment, covered the furniture, and scraped the paint off the windows. He came into class wearing a light-colored shirt, light pants—and he had a bad case of hives. "That's a good sign," I kidded him. "They mean you're literally *breaking out.*" Afterward, he began making progress as an actor. The last I heard of him, he was studying in England with the Royal Academy of Dramatic Arts.

Everyone is subject to having certain feelings triggered by different places. One restaurant may make you feel alive and joyful, while another may make you somber and sad. You may walk into a room and, without knowing why, immediately like the person who designed it. Or, you may instantly realize that you have nothing in common with that person. Knowing that you react this way should certainly allow you to understand how important it is to have any place you design accurately reflect your objective.

"Place" can be vital. In sports, players talk about the "home advantage." In business, the phrase "he's in my territory" is commonly used. The same actions, taken the same way, but in different places, have different results. An important business discussion is better conducted in the privacy of an office rather than in a crowded restaurant, but it is easier to break off a relationship in a crowded restaurant than in the privacy of a small room. Awareness of the "place" is crucial in choosing the right actions, as well as in the successful completion of those actions. Remember: The place can aid you in your actions. The place will affect you and your actions.

PLACE AND ACTION

Choose a place after stating your objective. Think of all the sensory aspects of the place you choose. Every place has a different degree of noise, attention-getting objects, smells, and opportunities to gain the full attention of another person.

If you can set up your own "place," make sure each room reflects precisely what you want it to. But make sure it reflects the real you, not an image you'd like other people to believe is the real you.

Be aware that other people have a distinct advantage when you are in their territory. They can manipulate the environment to their advantage.

Be aware that "place" is an extension of "self," and that you can immediately learn a great deal about a person from his home or office.

Don't try to overwhelm people with your place, or be overwhelmed by theirs. A place is like a set, it should be admired, then forgotten.

Don't use your place as a status symbol and fill it with all kinds of gizmos that state you're successful. Everything in your place should really be part of you.

A place can be anywhere you select. It can just as easily be a park bench as your bedroom, and it still can be used to your advantage.

Last, and perhaps most importnat, each place has a purpose. It is, above all, functional. Make sure every place you design serves the function it is intended to. It makes no sense to have a magnificent bedroom and an uncomfortable mattress.

Robert Edmond Jones wrote, "A setting is not just a beautiful thing, a collection of beautiful things. It is a presence, a mood, a warm wind fanning the drama to flame. It echoes, it enhances, it animates. It is an expectancy, a foreboding, a tension. It says nothing, but it gives everything."

Remember that the next time you are asked, "Your place or mine?"

CHAPTER TEN:
Opening Night—The Power Is in Performance

There are two good things in life, freedom of thought and freedom of action.

—W. SOMERSET MAUGHAM

Although theatre is often a reflection of life, in the end there is one great difference that sets them apart. And that is the ending.

On the stage, on screen, or on television, once the conclusion of the play, movie, or program is rehearsed, filmed, or taped, it will not change. No matter how often the same piece is played, the resolution will always be the same. Rhett Butler will always leave Scarlett O'Hara. Henry Higgins will always couple with Eliza Doolittle. And Kojak will always get his man, or woman. No matter how hard we wish some endings would change, Rocky Balboa will never become the heavyweight champion of the world. Only in sports events, games, and life is the ending flexible.

You can change your own life. You can determine your own future. You can set goals and learn new ways to achieve them. You can reintroduce feeling into your body again. And you can get what you want, from your supporting players, and from life. You can be the star of your own play.

Not everyone believes this. They *know* that fate has boxed them into a life situation that cannot be altered. They know their ending is already written, and it's just a matter of improvising the proper script dialogue until the final curtain rings down. They have, essentially, given up on themselves, their future, and their life.

If I told you now to tear this page out of this book, would you do it? Probably. Because, in reading these chapters, you have hopefully come to understand that attempting new and different actions is not only permissible, but desirable. By carefully selecting the actions that are most likely to succeed for you, you can gain control of your life.

Since you were a child, your producers, supporting characters, critics, even your audience, have tried to dictate your actions. They have limited what is possible by restricting you to a smaller number of permissible actions. Now that you are aware of that, and understand that the exercises in this book will help you deal with this problem, you should be able to lift these psychological barriers.

The only person still standing between you and the achievement of your basic objectives is the person closest to you right now. Yourself. Once you have determined your objectives, considered the possible paths to take and chosen one of them, and selected the specific actions that will lead you along that path, there remains only yourself to overcome. The mind stands like a guard, resisting anything that might upset the balance it has worked to create. And now you must bypass that guard and step into the uncharted territories of change.

One of the primary reasons people find it so difficult to

take control of their own future is their past. Too often, intelligent people allow past failures to prevent them from taking new actions that might cause great beneficial change in their lives. They project old movies in their mind, movies in which the ending was filmed long ago, and somehow believe that the ending can never be any different. They come to a new moment, a moment in which anything is possible, but they replay the old reel of a similiar event. They never attempt to meet new people because a new person rejected them in the past. They never confront the person who is bothering them because they tried to do that in the past and were embarrassed. They never try to do things in a new way because they tried it before and failed. Instead, they repeat the same actions they took in the old film, thereby guaranteeing that the ending will not change. They decide failure is their destiny, and then go about fulfilling it without complaint.

Most people have a whole collection of these home movies ready to be shown, each guaranteed to keep them caught in the same lifestyle. The "Failing with Strangers" epic is particularly popular. It is based on the true-life awkward adventures of a person probably long outgrown. There is another person you would really like to meet. I mean, *really*! But, in the past, every time you've tried to meet a new person you've become tongue-tied and red-faced. It happened when you were fourteen. It happened when you were eighteen. It happened again when you were twenty-one. And by the time you were twenty-three, it had happened again. Your attempts have always failed. No one has ever responded to you before, so it is obvious no one will respond to you in the future. It doesn't make any difference at all that you're twenty-nine, attractive, settled, and, in fact, nothing like you were at twenty-one. So you go through the motions, running the same old film. Sometimes it isn't even necessary to run the film—you just take a glimpse at the poster and knew you'll fail, so you don't even bother trying. And, just as sure as "Jaws" is going to be blown into pieces at the end of that film, you complete your own failure.

Old movies belong on late-night television, not in your life. All they do is put you in the proper frame of mind to repeat the same old failures. They allow you to convince yourself that you're going to fail even before you begin. The theories, exercises, and techniques contained in this book can be the basis for a brand-new, full-color production. They will allow you to learn how to adjust, and take control of situations, and not be bound by the failures of your past.

The exercises enable you to gain self-control, and that is a key element of change. If you cannot control your various parts, your emotions, mind, and body, then change will be almost impossible. The exercises will prove liberating. They will open up your awareness to your parts and your surroundings, and give you more of your self to control. More importantly, they will aid in the removal of the pent-up material, gathered over a lifetime of hurts, that is blocking your ability to completely open yourself to the possibilities of the world.

The value of the exercises is cumulative. The more you work with them, the more control you'll gain over your instrument. Following this chapter is a suggested schedule of exercise practice. Included in this schedule are some exercises not explained in chapters of this book. Use this schedule as a model to set up the most convenient routine for yourself. You can follow this schedule or make up one to fit your own day. The exercises are flexible, but it is necessary to continue working with them over a period of time. They will provide the groundwork that will eventually enable you to become free to act.

It does take time, as well as practice. You're breaking the habits of a lifetime. An actor may work at his craft for years before he is able to put everything he has learned into a role.

He must learn, practice, and finally test each aspect of his work, and only after he has mastered each particular aspect is he ready to incorporate them into his performance. In this book we have covered a great amount of information. Each part can be beneficial to you, but each is intended to be a part of a larger improvement program. Opening yourself to your emotions will help you feel better. Gaining control of your body will enable you to become more animate, more alive. Knowing how to choose effective actions will enable you to maintain control of yourself in various situations. And understanding that other people are trying to control your actions should prove liberating. But each of these is only a part of a much larger package. All of these aspects must be combined to enable you to put together a complete performance, to bring all of yourself, in the most complete way, to every moment.

How do you bring it all together? On the following pages, each step is carefully explained. By applying this method carefully, you should be able to make major changes in your life.

OBJECTIVES

Before you begin trying to change, you must know exactly what changes you want to make. What are your objectives? In order to do this, you must examine your current lifestyle and decide what is making you unhappy, or leaving you unsatisfied. Financial problems? Involvement or lack of involvement with another person? Your job? Your social life? Family problems? Guilt feelings? Whichever problems you identify should be used as a springboard to determine what you need or want. Your objective is your goal. It is the target you are aiming at, a means to measure your progress.

The more specific you can be in determing your objectives, the easier it will be to find the proper intentions and actions. Don't be general; "being happy" is not an objective. Getting a job with a better company, being cast into a role on Broadway, or even improving your social life are objectives. Knowing what you want will enable you to take advantage of the exercise work you are practicing, as well as the practical instruction on how to choose actions.

People create great difficulties for themselves by thinking in generalities. Instead of trying to reach an objective by taking many short, relatively easy steps, they attempt to do it in a few, often difficult advances. I was playing tennis recently and having trouble with my so-called game. Then I suddenly realized that tennis is played one stroke at a time. Instead of concentrating on the match as a whole, I brought all my attention to each individual shot. All I had to do was make sure I returned the ball once. Knowing this, I was able to play each shot to the best of my ability. Normally I let my desire to win overwhelm my game, but by breaking the match into smaller units, I was better able to concentrate on accomplishing each part. The single shots, of course, added up to the entire match.

Many young actors unsuccessfully beat their heads against stage doors trying to break into the theatre by being cast in a Broadway show. Their objective is to become a star. Instead of being specific about their objective, they generalize and end up taking extremely difficult actions. If their objective were more realistic, like getting a role in a play, they would open up numerous possibilities for themselves. The world of the theatre includes summer stock, regional theatres, dinner theatres, showcase productions, and bus and truck tours.

If your objective is to find a better job, be specific about what type of job you're looking for. If you want to meet someone new, try to decide what type of person you'd like to meet. Be as specific as possible about your objectives. This will help you to find your intentions more easily.

*   *   *

INTENTIONS

Once you've defined your objective, you have to figure out what steps you'll take to attain it. The steps you choose are your intentions. Your intention might be to charm someone, or to prove that you are capable of performing a certain job, or even to establish a relationship. Your intentions will constantly change as your situation changes. If you want to meet someone new, for example, you should first decide exactly what type of person you would feel most comfortable with. Knowing that, your first intention would be to decide where you would be most likely to meet that particular type of person. It might be a church group or a sleazy nightclub. Once there, your intention would become actually meeting another person who qualifies as the type you are looking for. After accomplishing that, it would be to charm that person, or dominate them, or entice them. As you accomplish each intention, you must select the next step.

Many people don't understand how to carry out their intentions clearly and completely. I see this problem frequently. My classes are almost always filled, and I audition each prospective student. Knowing that it is difficult to get into a class, these young actors and actresses come in for an interview already frightened that I won't accept them, or I won't like their type, or that I'll find something wrong with their character. And then they proceed to do all the wrong things.

Their desire is to get into my class. That is also their objective. Their intention should be to please me, or cajole, or impress, or anything that would make me want to immediately find a place for them. Instead, they manifest all the wrong intentions. They criticize, offend, or provoke. These people are often very responsive to the class, but if I didn't understand their original nervousness and insecurity, they would never be there in the first place.

We all get our intentions mixed up in life. Some relation-ships that grow to be vitally important begin on the worst possible footing, because people take actions that com-municate meanings far different from what they really in-tend to express.

Selecting the right intentions depends on your self-knowledge. The range of possible intentions is almost lim-itless, but you must be selective and base your choices on your type and character. The more you know about your-self, the easier it will be to select intentions that work for you. It makes no sense to have an intention to dominate if you are not capable of performing that type of action.

Through trial and error, you will be able to determine those intentions that will work for you. The range of inten-tions you can carry out should increase as you become aware of you character and continue to work on the exer-cises.

Intentions are like individual shots in a tennis match, they add up to equal your objective.

ACTIONS

To carry out your intentions, you take actions. Actions are the visual manifestation of all the preparations you've been making. If your long-range objective is to meet some-one you're compatible with, your immediate objective should be to find someone to date. Since you are an active, involved person, you want to meet someone who is also ac-tive and involved. You volunteer to work in a local political campaign. While working there, you spot someone who in-terests you. Your intention is to attract her attention. To do this, you must select an action. You can impress this per-son with your knowledge of politics, or please her by work-ing extremely hard, or interest her with your unique ideas. The purpose of each of these actions is to carry out your in-tention.

Determining which specific actions to take may well be the most important decision you will have to make. You must be capable of completing the actions you choose. Again, self-knowledge is extremely important. The more you know about yourself, the easier it will be to select workable actions. You must learn your strongest and weakest points, and try to stay within range of your strong points.

Once you decide what actions will convey your intention, you should start being selective. Consider the people you'll be dealing with and the place in which you will act. Learn as much as possible about "place" and other types of characters so you will be aware of everything that might be available to you in carrying out your actions, as well as what possible actions might be taken to oppose you.

By asking a few questions of other people, for example, you might learn that the person who interests you wants to run for elective office someday. Your actions will be to be supportive of this desire. You might flatter this person, or suggest ways you can aid her, or display a knowledge of political work.

As mentioned before, "place" can be an important factor in the success or failure of your actions. If your action is to be commanding, for example, you would walk into an office and take the biggest or centrally located chair. But if you were trying to flatter someone, you might make sure they are seated in the central position.

REHEARSALS

Once you decide how you will put your intention into actions, it is possible to actually rehearse for the event. The event is what I call the actually carrying out of the action. Since your actions may be opposed by the actions of another person or by the elements, you can prepare for that just as an actor prepares for his role in a play.

Your rehearsals really began the moment you began reading this book. Everything you've learned is preparation for your performance. But, to rehearse for a specific performance, do just as an actor does, actually perform your part. Start by creating a sense memory of the person you will be dealing with, if you know who it is, or the type of person, if you don't know specifically. Use all the techniques you learned earlier.

When you make this personalization, try to imagine the atmosphere of the place in which you'll be meeting. Is it a public place? Will the background noise be loud or soft? Is it garish or intimate? Obviously you will not be able to create the entire scene in your mnd, but imagining the setting will make your personalization more valuable. Now, speak to that person, your boss, your wife, your date, the internal revenue investigator, an employee you have to fire, the neighbor you're finally going to tell off, the bank official from whom you're requesting a loan, a potential employer, a manager of a department store's complaint department, just as you intend to when you actually confront them. If your action will be demanding, speak to them in a demanding voice. Use your whole body to demand exactly what you want. If you are going to be gentle, speak to this person from that condition. Try to find the proper words to convey your action. But if you can't, select an appropriate monolgue from this or another book. Use the same voice and mannerisms you'll be using during your performance.

Imagine the reactions this person might have, and try switching actions to suit them. If possible, find someone to play the role of the person or people you'll be dealing with. This will give you an opportunity to really rehearse your part. It can also be fun. In class we occasionally have one student play the part of an agent or casting director and allow another student to practice the actions they would use to try to be signed with this agent, or to gain an audition for a particular part. The student playing the agent or director intentionally switches his actions, throwing new and difficult situations at the other students. He may sympathize at first, then resist, then encourage. This type of rehearsal teaches students to react to changing actions, mostly through trial and error. With someone else's help, you can rehearse at home and be ready to repeat your performance during the real event.

Nothing improves without practice, and you can improve the effectiveness of your actions through this type of practice. There are no risks involved. There will be no acceptance or rejection as a result of these practice sessions. Generally people don't attempt new actions, because they lack experience with them. They have no idea how to take the action, how to command, how to evoke concern, how to provoke anger. Often, they don't even know where to start. Through practice you can discover where you'll have difficulty and what actions you are not capable of utilizing. These sessions will enhance your self-knowledge and self-control.

Some sports skills can be practiced alone. You can hit a tennis ball or throw a rubber ball against a wall. You can shoot a basketball or drive a golf ball by yourself. Swimming and bowling are individual sports. You can get into shape, learn how to move, improve your strength and stamina, and work on specific problems by yourself. You may practice a basketball shot or a swimming turn five thousand times before gaining enough confidence to attempt it in competition. But if you don't practice, you'll never improve your game. These imaginary personalizations, these practice sessions, are rehearsals for life. They will pay off for you. If you work, they work.

PERFORMANCE

Everything you have learned in this book should be used to present a consummate performance. You should have an objective, selected intentions, and know your probable actions. To carry out those actions completely, you should consider the place, the objectives of the people you will have to deal with, and their possible actions. In carrying out your actions, you should utilize your costume, mannerisms, voice, and emotional condition. The more you are able to bring all of these things into play, the more completely you will achieve your intentions. If you learn how to bring all of these aspects of yourself together, you should be able to make important changes in your life.

There is, however, a problem you will share with actors: nerves. Actors, at times, become so nervous they forget their lines. People become so nervous, or tense, they forget all they have worked out and rehearsed. They forget their intentions, the actions they've planned, and instead fall back into the safe, fixed position they have occupied for so long. They lose confidence and become comfortable in their discomfort. This is known as stage fright.

Actors use numerous devices to recall their lines. They might pick up a cue from the stage manager or another actor, they might have written key words on their costumes or props, they might even invent an excuse to temporarily leave the stage. Some actors invent new lines. If they know their intention, they can successfully improvise.

If you're like most people, you don't write on your clothing, travel with a stage manager, or even have your intended actions written down. But you can use keys. By returning to the beginning, you can recall exactly what you are trying to do. The beginning is the one fixed point you are always sure of, the subject of our first exercise, your breath. No matter how nervous, embarrassed, or confused you become, you can always return to your breath. When you remember to bring attention to your breathing, you will be reminded that you have an objective, intentions, and actions, and exactly what they are. This attention can also serve to remind you to utilize the place you are in and all available props to further your intention. Your breath is the thread that holds together the beads of your objective.

Every action you take during a performance will have meaning. The chair you choose to sit in, the way you sit—upright or slouched—whether you smoke or not, the notes you take, the words you use to answer questions, the questions you ask. Absolutely everything counts, and you should attempt to use everything available to you. Remember, every single action should serve to reinforce your intention.

During your performance, it is imperative that you pay close attention to the changing actions of the supporting players. By determining their objectives before the event, you'll be aware of the actions they are attempting—even though they may not be aware that they have an intention or are taking actions—and you may be able to find the proper actions to counter theirs.

Life is only haphazard if you allow it to be.

To approach an event, a performance, in this way, rather than allowing "fate" to simply take control of your life, is the most sincere way to live. It enables you to apply all of yourself to your intention. This is total involvement, and no one can require any more of you than that.

Sometimes, though, even the biggest, brassiest, most expensive Broadway shows are dismal flops. Producers spent a small fortune reconstructing an entire theatre to fit around a dirt road for a play called *Dude*. It was put together by a talented group of people, each of whom had enjoyed big Broadway successes. It was a million dollar production—and earned its place in theatrical history by becoming one of the most expensive flops of all time. Sometimes your performance might flop, too, but, unlike the producers of *Dude*, you have many opportunities to try again. Although many people share the belief that when something doesn't work the first time, it will never work, this is not true. Every performance is not opening night. The critics are not always poised with poison pencils ready to tear you down for every mistake. Your life is a long-running production, and your performance can constantly be improved.

You are working toward making major changes in your life. In doing this, you will suffer some defeats. The important thing is to gain knowledge from these attempts. This is a learned technique. To learn, you must be willing to take some risks and suffer some losses. When something does go wrong for you, examine your performance for mistakes, as you would a score sheet. Exactly what went wrong? Did you choose the wrong actions? Did you attempt those actions in the wrong way? Was the place wrong for the type of actions you selected? Did the other person take actions you were not able to respond to? There is a reason for every failure. Instead of simply accepting defeat and attributing it to fate, break the event down into its component parts, just as you built up for it, and find out exactly where and why you failed.

Actors get in trouble when they cannot get out of generalities, when they cannot diagnose the problems they have. It takes no expertise to know there is a problem, to know you are not as successful as you'd like to be, or are not happy, or satisfied. But you have to figure out why. Without knowing specifically what is wrong, it is impossible to make the proper corrections.

Once you have determined the problem, work on that component. If it is the place, either change the place or find new actions that will conform to that place. In acting, breaking down a role into its parts is called technique. That involves recognizing that a problem exists, discovering what the problem is, and solving that problem. Through practice, you can improve your technique in life.

Obviously you cannot prepare for every event as I've described. Every moment in life does not involve a performance. Sometimes important meetings or opportunities occur without any warning, without allowing you a chance to prepare your role for that event. With enough "pregame" practice, specific preparation won't be necessary. The method outlined in this book is a way of learning how to improve your life. It brings more of you into the world, and opens more of the world to you. The more you work with this method, the more natural it will become. Eventually you will become aware of which actions work best for you and learn to concentrate on using them. You will know what your type is, and how best to utilize your character to promote yourself with your supporting characters.

This is a technique. It can be learned. It can be practiced. It can become part of your life. Once you free your emotions and gain control over your body and mind, you will be able to bring yourself completely to any moment, to take the actions necessary to achieve your desires, to get exactly what you want.

You will become free to act.

The Exercise Program

Practice is the best of all instructors.

—VIRGIL

Following is a suggested schedule of exercises for an average week. The value of the exercises is cumulative. The more you work with them, the more effective they will be for you. There is no point at which you will be able to say, "finished," any more than you will ever really become a "finished" human being. You are constantly developing, and these exercises will serve as an aid in that growth.

It is important to remember that this is only a suggested program. There is no right or wrong here. This is not the single correct way of combining all the exercise material. It is, rather, a means of showing a complete program. You should take all the exercise work we've dealt with in this book and organize your own program consistent with your own lifestyle.

In many instances, I have not repeated the complete in-

210

structions for each exercise. Where a page is noted, reread indicated material before beginning the exercise.

Do each exercise until you feel you have completed it. As long as you continue to gain benefits from it, continue to do it.

It will be helpful, but it is not necessary, to make an exercise chart of your own. Indicate what exercises you are doing, on what days, and for what length of time. An exercise may take five minutes or an hour. Only you can determine how long it takes for a particular exercise to be effective for you.

You should begin realizing certain results immediately. The sensory exercises, in particular, should help make you more aware of your surroundings and the people in your life as soon as you begin working with them. The personalizations will take a little longer, but once you are able to draw real feelings, progress will come quickly.

If *you* work, this exercise program will work.

MONDAY

Relaxation Exercise: (Page 67) Scanning attention to total body.

Sensory Exercise: (Page 73) Hot or cold liquid (coffee, cocoa, tea, milk, juice).

Flow easily from relaxation exercise into sensory exercise. Explore shape, design, and color of container of liquid. Explore warmth or coolness. Then smell and taste. Examine weight and texture of container and muscles and movement of body in handling it. Hold palm to and above container to feel steam, effervescence, condensation. Experience temperature and texture with fingertips. Keep attention on entire body so as to use only those muscles and movements necessary to deal with object. Conserve energy.

No waste. Give attention to liquid as it flows inside the body after drinking.

Now do all this in your imagination, giving attention to all the details experienced with actual object.

Personalization: (Page 47) Recall someone you loved very much who hurt and/or angered you. Choose actions to *demand,* to *criticize,* to *challenge.* Then choose actions with the same personalization to *plead,* to *appeal,* to *give affection.*

Gestures and Body Language: (Page 122) Bring attention periodically to the movements and manner in which you converse with your hands and body. Noncritical observation.

Color Exercise: Bring attention to the color red in the environment as you travel to and from work or while traveling from one place to another.

Dress: Make one slight alteration in your attire or your mode of personal grooming.

*Practice returning to breath

TUESDAY

Relaxation Exercise: Scanning attention to total body.

Sensory Exercise: Inanimate object with sharp taste (sweetness, sourness)—a lemon, hot pepper, strawberry, green apple, etc.

(Same instructions as Monday sensory exercise, excluding hot or cold temperature aspects.)

Personalization: Recall an authority figure who wielded great influence over you. Choose actions to *confront,* to *challenge,* to *admonish,* to *rebuke,* to *mock,* to *protest.*

Then choose actions to *implore*, to *plead*, to *beg*, to *compromise*.

Color Exercise: Same as Monday, with color green. Wink at one homely person.

Dress: Change order in habitual sequence of dressing.

Voice: Periodically bring attention to quality and rhythms of your voice during day's interactions. Noncritical observation.

*Practice returning to breath

WEDNESDAY

Relaxation Exercise: Same as Monday.

Sensory Exercise: Explore an object with a sharp smell— flowers, bar of soap, aromatic wood (pine, cedar), perfume, herbs, fruit, or vegetable. Same instructions as Monday and Tuesday.

Personalization: Recall person you were very attracted to, excited by, but didn't consummate relationship with. Choose actions to *charm*, to *excite*, to *command*, to *titillate*, to *allure*, to *flirt*, and any other action you were incapable of.

Color Exercise: Choose color blue in environment. Same as Monday and Tuesday.

Dress: Include one new "prop" with your attire. Try to utilize it in your commerce with others. Wear a piece of clothing you usually would never associate with your "character."

*Practice returning to breath.

THURSDAY

Relaxation Exercise: Same as Monday.

Sensory Exercise: Explore materials of different textures—fur, silk, corduroy, burlap, etc. Experience materials on different parts of body—face, neck, arms, stomach, thighs, feet, etc.

Body: Periodically bring attention to motions of your body, the way you walk, sit, stand, handle objects. Nonjudgmental observations.

Choose one person you spend time around and observe his/her characteristics.

Personalization: Recall someone you were very frightened of. Choose intentions to *contest,* to *accost,* to *defy,* to *attack,* to *repulse.*

Dress: Try to define the most important aspect of your habitual dress. Then change it today or innovate from it. As you interact with others, try to include the use of all your accessories (jewelry, etc.) in your body language. Let others be complimented by and be supportive of your body discourse.

*Practice returning to your breath.

FRIDAY

Relaxation Exercise: Same as Monday.

Sensory Exercise: Sound. Explore container of hot or cold liquid (same as Monday), only now include a spoon for stirring and intermittently tap spoon against container and bring sensory attention to sound. As you do this, include the other sounds that happen to be in the environment during the exercise.

Body: Selectively try to sit and walk in ways contrary to your habitual patterns.

Animal Exercise: (Page 107)

Personalization: Recall a time when you most needed help, when you felt most helpless. Choose a person you wanted most to turn to for support or understanding. Select intentions to *appeal,* to *implore,* to *plead.* Then change intentions to *demand,* to *compel.*

Dress: Choose one piece of clothing totally opposite to your "type" and wear it for the day. I dare you.

*Practice returning to your breath.

Monologues

The monologues in this section are to be used for personalizations when you simply cannot find your own words. You should find your own emotions, then speak them through the words of the great playwrights included in this section. The actual words themselves are not important. This is not an acting exercise, so it is not necessary to understand the complete context of the plays from which they are taken. These exercises have been selected because they have proven to be of great help in expressing certain emotions.

You can have a great deal of fun with these monologues. In essence, you will be acting; you will be injecting your own emotions into another person's words. But your reason for doing this is not to entertain an audience, but rather to feel the emotion. Get into these monologues. Scream and shout; be loving; be nasty. This is an opportunity to act in a way you've never allowed yourself to act before, without any chance of punishment. Enjoy it. It will be of great benefit to you.

And, while you are doing this, be aware of the emotions you are feeling.

It is not necessary to spend time memorizing this material. Use the book, but try to read through the monologue a few times before attempting the personalization, so you will not stumble during your exercise.

Once you learn to summon your inner emotions, these monologues will no longer be necessary. Your own words expressing these feelings will spout out of you spontaneously.

MONOLOGUE from *MADAME COLOMBE*—Anhouilh

(To resist) I support myself now . . . I like the way I live. When something amuses me I laugh without worrying whether you'll think it's funny or start to sulk as soon as we get home . . . I don't have to hurt you anymore. We've both suffered plenty from your always being hurt. . . *(To dare)* Would you like me to be honest with you? *(To reprove)* I've been very happy since you went away. Every morning when I wake up the sun is shining. I look out the window and for the first time in years there's no tragedy in the street. *(To intrigue)* And if the mailman rings I go the the door in my nightgown . . . there's no drama. I'm not a loose woman . . . we're just a woman and a mailman happy with each other . . . he, because he gets a kick out of seeing me in my nightgown I, because I've given him a little pleasure. *(To admonish)* I like the whole business . . . being attractive and nibbling breakfast while I do the housework and washing myself in the kitchen sink naked with the window open. And if the old man from across the way runs for his opera glasses, I can't get excited and cry for two hours trying to calm you down.

(To dismiss) You'll never know, my darling, how uncomplicated life can be without you.

MONOLOGUE from *A DOLL'S HOUSE*—Henrik Ibsen

(To repel) You neither think nor talk like the man I could bind myself to. As soon as your fear was over—and it was not fear for what threatened me, but for what might happen to you—when the whole thing was past, as far as you were concerned it was exactly as if nothing at all had happened. *(To mock)* Exactly as before, I was your little skylark, your doll, which you would in future treat with doubly gentle care, because it was so brittle and fragile. *(To defy)* Torvald—it was then it dawned upon me that for eight years I had been living here with a strange man, and had borne him three children—. *(To assault)* Oh, I can't bear to think of it! I could tear myself into little bits!

(To caution) I have heard that when a wife deserts her husband's house, as I am doing now, he is legally freed from all your obligations toward her. *(To command)* In any case I set you free from all your obligations. You are not to feel yourself bound in the slightest way, any more than I shall. There must be perfect freedom on both sides. See here is your ring back. Give me mine.

MONOLOGUE from *ENEMIES*—Maxim Gorky

(To appeal) I feel uncomfortable up there in front of those people, with their cold eyes saying, 'Oh, we know all that, it's old, it's boring!' *(To implore)* I feel weak and defenceless in front of them, I can't capture them, I can't excite them. . . . *(To arouse)* I long to tremble in front of them with fear, with joy, to speak words full of fire and passion and anger, words that cut like knives, that burn like torches . . . *(To excite)* I want to throw armfuls of words, throw them bounteously, abundantly, terrifyingly . . . so that people are set alight by them and, shout aloud, and turn to flee from them . . . *(To impassion)* And then I'll stop them. Toss them different words. Words beautiful as flowers.

Words full of hope, and joy, and love. And they'll all be weeping, and I'll weep too . . . wonderful tears. *(To inspire)* They applaud. Smother me with flowers. Bear me up on their shoulders. For a moment—I hold sway over them all . . . Life is there, in that one moment all of life, in a single moment.

MONOLOGUE from *SAINT JOAN*—George Bernard Shaw

(To challenge) Yes: they told me you were fools, and that I was not to listen to your fine words nor trust to your charity. You promised me my life; but you lied. *(To scold)* You think that life is nothing but not being stone dead. It is not the bread and water I fear: I can live on bread: when have I asked for more? It is no hardship to drink water if the water be clean. Bread has no sorrow for me, and water no affliction. *(To shame)* But to shut me from the light of the sky and the sight of the fields and flowers; to chain my feet so that I can never again ride with the soldiers nor climb the hills; to make me breathe foul damp darkness and keep from me everything that brings me back to the love of God when your wickedness and foolishness tempt me to hate Him: all this is worse than the furnace in the Bible that was heated seven times. *(To oppose)* I could do without my warhorse; I could drag about in a skirt; I could let the banners and the trumpets and the knights and soldiers pass me and leave me behind as they leave the other women, *(To appeal)* if only I could still hear the wind in the trees, the larks in the sunshine, the young lambs crying through the healthy frost, and the blessed church bells that send my angel voices floating to me on the wind. *(To defy)* But without these things I cannot live; and by your wanting to take them away from me, or from any human creature, I know that your counsel is of the devil, and that mine is of God.

MONOLOGUE from *CYRANO* DE *BERGERAC*— Edmond Rostand

(To tempt)
Yes, that is Love—that wind
Of terrible and jealous beauty, blowing
Over me—that dark fire, that music . . .
Yet
(To reassure)
Love seeketh not his own! Dear, you may take
My happiness to make you happier,
Even though you never know I gave it you—
(To get compassion)
Only let me hear sometimes, all alone,
The distant laughter of your joy! . . .
(To stir)
I never
Look at you, but there's some new virtue born
In me, some new courage. Do you begin
To understand, a little? Can you feel
My soul, there in the darkness, breathe on you?
(To thrill)
—Oh, but to-night, now, I dare say these things—
I . . . to you . . . and you hear them! . . . It is too much!
In my most sweet unreasonable dreams,
I have not hoped for this!

MONOLOGUE from *WHO'S AFRAID OF VIR- GINIA WOOLF?*—Edward Albee

(To demean) Well, maybe you're right, baby. You can't come together with nothing, and you're nothing! *(To intimidate)* SNAP! It went snap tonight at Daddy's party. I sat there at Daddy's party, and I watched you . . . I watched you sitting there, and I watched the younger men around

you, the men who were going to go somewhere. *(To humili-ate)* And I sat there and I watched you, and you weren't there! And it snapped! It finally snapped! *(To bombard)* And I'm going to howl it out, and I'm not going to give a damn what I do, and I'm going to make the damned biggest explosion you ever heard.

MONOLOGUE from *A DOLL'S HOUSE*—Henrik
        Ibsen

(To confront) But it was absolutely necessary that he should not know! My goodness, can't you understand that? It was necessary he should have no idea what a dangerous condition he was in. *(To entreat)* It was to me that the doctors came and said that his life was in danger, and that the only thing to save him was to live in the south. *(To implore)* Do you suppose I didn't try, first of all, to get what I wanted as if it were for myself? I told him how much I should love to travel abroad like other young wives; I tried tears and entreaties with him; I told him that he ought to remember the condition I was in, and that he ought to be kind and indulgent to me; *(To alarm)* I even hinted that he might raise a loan. That nearly made him angry, Christine. He said I was thoughtless, and that it was his duty as my husband not to indulge me in my whims and caprices—as I believe he called them. *(To exalt)* Very well, I thought, you must be saved—and that was how I came to devise a way out of the difficulty—

MONOLOGUE from *SCENES FROM AMERICAN
        LIFE*—A. R. Gurney, Jr.

(To object) I'm very sorry, but this year I don't think I'll cough up another nickel for Yale. I'm distressed that the library was burned but why should I keep Yale up when even

its own students persist in dragging her down? *(To implore)* Indeed, why do people like you and me and Snoozer, Brad, have to keep things up all the time? It seems to me I spend most of my time keeping things up. *(To protest)* I keep the symphony up. I keep the hospital up. I keep our idiotic local theatre up. *(To challenge)* I keep my lawn up because no one else will. I keep my house up so the children will want to come home someday. I keep the summer house up for grandchildren. I keep up all that furniture Mother left me because Sally won't keep it up. I even keep my morals up despite all sorts of immediate temptations. *(To attack)* I keep my chin up, I keep my faith up, I keep my dander up in this grim world. And I'm sick, sick, SICK of it. I'm getting tired supporting all those things that maybe ought to collapse. Sometimes all I think I am is an old jock strap, holding up the sagging balls of the whole damn WORLD!

MONOLOGUE from DESIRE UNDER THE
        ELMS—Eugene O'Neill

(To tease) Ye don't mean that, Eben. Ye may think ye mean it, mebbe, but ye don't. *(To lure)* Ye can't. It's agin nature, Eben. Ye been fightin' yer nature ever since the day I come—tryin' t'tell yerself I hain't purty t'ye. *(To arouse)* Hain't the sun strong an' hot? Ye kin feel it burnin' into the earth—Nature—makin' thin's grow—into somethin' else— till ye're jined with it—an' it's your'n—but it owns ye, too— an' makes ye grow bigger—like a tree—like them elums. *(To taunt)*—Nature'll beat ye, Eben. Ye might's well own up t'it fust 's last.

MONOLOGUE from *MISS JULIE*—August Strindberg

(To contest) You don't think I can bear the sight of blood. You think I'm so weak. *(To torment)* Oh, how I should like

to see your blood and your brains on a chopping-block! I'd like to see the whole of your sex swimming like that in a sea of blood. *(To attack)* I think I could drink out of your skull, bathe my feet in your broken breast and eat your heart roasted whole. *(To challenge)* You think I'm weak. You think I love you, that my womb yearned for your seed and I want to carry your offspring under my heart and nourish it with my blood.